Hiya . . .

Have you ever wanted to change the world? Coco Tanberry reckons she might just be able to do it, armed only with an old violin, a fluffy panda hat, a rucksack full of cupcakes and a LOT of determination. Sadly, she has reckoned without surly loner Lawrie Marshall, who seems to think everything she does is ridiculous. When the two of them find themselves working together to rescue some ill-treated ponies, there's bound to be trouble . . .

Coco is a tomboy with big plans and bucketfuls of enthusiasm. She cares so much about so many things and wants to fix them all, but she's impulsive – she doesn't always think before she acts. While she's busy trying to save the world, her own family is falling to pieces – but Coco can't help the big sister she loves without drawing attention to herself and the tangle of lies and deceit she has woven to hide the dangerous risks she is taking.

Coco reminds me a lot of myself back at the age of twelve. I am still crazy about animals and hate injustice of any kind . . . and like Coco, if I thought I could save the world with cake, I'd definitely give it my best shot!

Coco Caramel is the fourth book in the Chocolate Box Girls series . . . a story of growing up and finding the courage to do the right thing, even if the 'right thing' turns out to be a little different from what you first imagined. Curl up with a cool chocolate milkshake and let the adventure begin . . .

Cathy Cassidy xxx

Cathy Cassidy

COCO Caramel

the chocolate box girls

PUFFIN

PUFFIN BOOKS

Published by the Penguin Group
Penguin Books Ltd, 80 Strand, London WC2R ORL, England
Penguin Group (USA) Inc., 375 Hudson Street, New York, New York 10014, USA
Penguin Group (Canada), 90 Eglinton Avenue East, Suite 700, Toronto, Ontario, Canada M4P 2Y3
(a division of Pearson Penguin Canada Inc.)
Penguin Ireland, 25 St Stephen's Green, Dublin 2, Ireland (a division of Penguin Books Ltd)
Penguin Group (Australia), 707 Collins Street, Melbourne, Victoria 3008, Australia
(a division of Pearson Australia Group Pty Ltd)
Penguin Books India Pvt Ltd, 11 Community Centre, Panchsheel Park, New Delhi – 110 017, India
Penguin Group (NZ), 67 Apollo Drive, Rosedale, Auckland 0632, New Zealand
(a division of Pearson New Zealand Ltd)
Penguin Books (South Africa) (Pty) Ltd, Block D, Rosebank Office Park, 181 Jan Smuts Avenue, Parktown
North, Gauteng 2193, South Africa

Penguin Books Ltd, Registered Offices: 80 Strand, London WC2R ORL, England

puffinbooks.com

First published 2013
Published in this edition
015
All rights reserved

Text copyright © Cathy Cassidy, 2013
Illustrations copyright © Puffin Books, 2013
Illustrations by Sara Chadwick-Holmes

The moral right of the author and illustrator has been asserted

Set in Baskerville MT Std
Typeset by Palimpsest Book Production Ltd, Falkirk, Stirlingshire
Printed and bound in Great Britain by Clays Ltd, Elcograf S.p.A.

British Library Cataloguing in Publication Data
A CIP catalogue record for this book is available from the British Library

ISBN: 978-0-141-34159-0

www.greenpenguin.co.uk

Thanks . . .

To Liam, Cal and Caitlin for being generally awesome, and to Mum, Joan, Andy, Lori and all of my fab family. Thanks to Helen, Sheena, Fiona, Jessie, Lal and Maggi for the hugs, the chocolate and the pep talks, and to all of my lovely friends for putting up with me.

Thanks to Ruth my ever-patient PA, to maths-guru Martyn and to my brilliant agent Darley and his team. Hugs to Alex, my editor, and Amanda too; also to Sara for the stunning artwork. Huge thanks to Adele, Jayde, Julia, Emily, Samantha, Helen and all of the creative, clever team at Puffin.

Special thanks to Roy and Jean for letting me borrow their names for the story. Jean ran the riding school I went to back when I was nine; I had zero talent at riding, but Roy and Jean have been much loved family friends all these years. Last but not least, thanks to all my lovely, loyal readers – YOU make all the hard work worthwhile!

1

They say that families are like chocolate — mostly sweet, with a few nuts. More than a few, in my family's case . . . and they say that I'm the crazy one? Yeah, right.

They also say that life is like a box of chocolates, and that you can't expect every one you pick to be exactly the way you'd like it to be. This seems a little ridiculous to me – and as my mum and my stepdad Paddy run a chocolate business, well . . . I think I should know. Better just to pick out your favourites, even if they don't come in a fancy box. With a little planning, you can get what you want, with no nasty surprises. Simple.

I lean back against the tree trunk and rest my violin across my lap.

I have just finished my practice. I have only been playing

❀❀❀❀❀❀❀❀❀❀❀❀❀❀❀❀❀❀❀❀❀

for a year and because my family is not especially musical and not especially tolerant of beginner violinists, I am banned from playing indoors.

Our house, Tanglewood, is a B&B, and Mum says that my playing might disturb the guests, and that she cannot afford to lose custom because of it. This shows you the kind of thing I have to put up with because only one or two guests actually complained, and that was *ages* ago, when I was just starting out. These days I am lots better and my playing sounds nothing at all like cats being strangled.

The B&B business is winding down a little lately now that the chocolate business is taking off, so why anyone cares about losing one or two guests who are probably tone-deaf anyway is quite beyond me. Still, I am banished from the house and so I have to practise outside, perched in my favourite climbing tree, an oak. It is quite a comfortable tree because there is a wide branch that meets the main trunk almost at a right angle. I have added a cushion from one of the garden chairs, and if you want to you can pull your legs up and lean back as if you are sitting in a lumpy old armchair.

❀❀❀❀❀❀❀❀❀❀❀❀❀❀❀❀❀❀❀❀❀❀❀❀

Or you can let your legs dangle, the way I am right now, and look down through the oak leaves at the ground below. It is October, the end of the half-term break, and the leaves are a hundred shades of gold and burnt orange and crimson. There is a definite chill in the air, and I am wearing a scarf, a jumper and a beanie hat. It's not quite cold enough yet for gloves, but it will be soon. If you have ever tried playing a violin wearing red and black striped woolly gloves, you will know that this is not good.

You'd think my family would take pity on me and let me practise indoors, but there's no chance of that. Sometimes I think they are philistines.

My friends at school think my family is cool, but they don't know the half of it. Mum and Paddy are always hassled and busy, juggling B&B stuff with chocolate orders and new truffle ideas and designs for the handpainted boxes. As for having four sisters . . . well, that can be seriously hard work, especially when you are the youngest.

Like I said, my family is mostly nuts.

Honey, my eldest sister, is definitely more sour than sweet – she looks cute on the outside, but inside she's pure rebel. It's like she has no limits, no rules. She

3

accidentally caused a fire back in the summer and tried to run away; a few weeks after, she stayed out all night and skipped the first day of school. Everyone thought she'd run away again and the police and social services got involved. Scary stuff. Honey seems to have quietened down again now, but for how long?

My stepsister Cherry is cool, but when she first arrived last year, she had a few problems sorting fact from fiction. She also had a problem staying away from Honey's boyfriend, and now the two of them are an item. This is great for Cherry, but not so great for Honey – since Shay ditched Honey she has dated practically every boy in Somerset, the more unsuitable the better. Cherry and Shay broke up recently for a week, and rumour had it that Honey was responsible . . . but they're back together now and stronger than ever. Don't get me wrong, I like Cherry a lot, but still, I can't help wishing she hadn't fallen for Shay Fletcher.

So. My sister Skye likes to dress in dead girls' dresses, or 'vintage' as she calls it. Last year she had a crush on some imaginary ghost boy; this year she has a long-distance boyfriend up in London, and they are always

4

writing and texting and emailing. If you want my opinion, I think she should have stuck with the ghost boy.

As for Summer, Skye's twin – I used to think she had it all; looks, talent, popularity, big dreams, determination. She had a scholarship for a boarding ballet school this term . . . but she threw it all away, cracked under the pressure. Her dream turned into a nightmare, and she is still struggling to break free of it. These days, Summer is like a shadow girl, frail, fragile, lost. She picks at her food as if she thinks it could be poisoned, and we have to creep around her pretending nothing is wrong when we all know that things are very wrong indeed.

Summer hangs out the whole time with Alfie Anderson, who is a million miles from cool, the kind of boy who puts salt instead of sugar in your hot chocolate and thinks it's funny. I really don't, and I have no idea what Summer sees in him.

Boys are nothing but trouble – if they vanished off the face of the earth right now, Honey, Cherry, Skye and Summer would probably be a whole lot happier and much more fun. Personally, I think animals are far more reliable and rewarding.

✿✿✿✿✿✿✿✿✿✿✿✿✿✿✿✿✿✿✿✿✿✿✿

I peer down through the leaves at Fred the dog, who is waiting patiently at the foot of the tree, while Humbug my pet sheep munches grass nearby. You see? Animals are loyal. They don't care if you play a few dud notes when practising the violin. They never judge you, and they don't let you down.

People can learn a lot from animals. I know that my sisters are not perfect, but I love them and I am loyal to them. If someone else says anything at all against them, I will defend them to my last breath.

The problem with being the youngest is that people don't take you seriously. You are stuck forever as the baby of the family, which can be very annoying indeed. I'll show them, though. I have my life all planned out and I am pretty sure it's going to be *amazing*.

I want to work with animals – I will do voluntary work and save endangered species. I have started on this task already because let's face it, time is running out. I am having a cake sale at school on Monday, in aid of endangered pandas, and before half-term I started a petition to save the white rhino. I collected 233 signatures, and sent them all off to the government with a first-class stamp.

❀❀❀❀❀❀❀❀❀❀❀❀❀❀❀❀❀❀❀❀❀❀❀❀

Once I have saved the panda, the white rhino and a bunch of other threatened animals, I will train to be a vet and eventually I will live in a big house by the sea (a bit like Tanglewood) and have my own horses and play the violin whenever I like. Indoors and out.

I know what I want, and it doesn't seem too much to ask.

If life is a box of chocolates, I will just make sure that I pick carefully. Why waste time on nougat and jaw-breaking toffee brittle when you can have something you really love instead? I like most of the truffles that my stepdad Paddy makes for his business, The Chocolate Box, but the caramel truffle he invented for me back on my twelfth birthday a while ago is without a doubt the best of all.

If my life is going to be a box of chocolates, I will plan ahead and make sure I choose caramel, rich and smooth and sweet, every time.

30p or 4 for £1

2

I set up a table in the foyer of Exmoor Park Middle School, cover it with a red and white checked cloth and drape my handpainted banner, *Save the Giant Panda*, across the front of it. Then I set out the plates and arrange my home-baked cupcakes, which I have iced with little black and white panda faces. Who could resist?

'They look better than the whale ones you made last time,' my friend Sarah comments. 'These ones are actually quite cute. What are we charging? Ten pence? Twenty pence?'

'Thirty pence, or two for fifty pence,' I decide. 'It's for charity, isn't it?'

It is the first day back after the October holiday and Sarah and I have been allowed out of history ten minutes early to set up our stall, so that we can make the most of the breaktime rush once the bell goes.

Sarah unpacks a plastic box of chocolate fridge cake and I set out a slightly dented Victoria sponge, a tin of chocolate crispy cakes and a tub of rock buns that are a little too rock-like for comfort. My friends always rally round at times like this and manage to contribute something. I arrange my handmade leaflets, explaining why the giant panda is endangered and needs our help. I have learnt the hard way that my fellow pupils are rarely impressed by my efforts to raise funds with sponsored walks or silences. They are much more likely to part with their cash if cake is involved.

'OK,' Sarah says. 'Thirty seconds and counting. Watch out for those Year Six boys, I'm sure they nicked my flapjacks last time!'

'Nobody will dare swipe so much as a crumb while I'm watching,' I promise.

I pull on my fake-fur panda hat with the sticky-up ears and square my shoulders, ready to do battle.

'Here we go,' I say to Sarah. 'For the pandas!'

The bell rings and the foyer floods with kids. They can scent cake, and they swarm round the stall, grabbing panda cupcakes and wedges of Victoria sponge, shoving warm, sticky coins into the collection tin.

One cute little Year Five girl buys up the whole tin of chocolate crispy cakes for £5 because it's her mum's birthday. Then I spot a weaselly Year Six boy trying to pocket a couple of chunks of chocolate fridge cake and grab his wrist firmly. 'Fifty pence, please,' I say sweetly. 'All proceeds go to help the giant panda!'

'Help it do what?' he asks, reluctantly handing over his cash.

'Survive,' I explain patiently. 'They are almost extinct because bamboo forests are being cut down and pandas eat mainly bamboo shoots.'

'Why don't they eat something different then?' the kid asks. 'Fish 'n' chips. Big Macs. Chocolate fridge cake.'

I roll my eyes. 'They can't,' I explain. 'They are *pandas*, not people. They are supposed to eat bamboo shoots, and people are destroying their habitat. It's up to us to save them!'

The boy's face hardens. 'If that's true, you really shouldn't wear a panda hat,' he says. 'That's just sick.' He walks away, scoffing fridge cake.

❀❀❀❀❀❀❀❀❀❀❀❀❀❀❀❀❀❀❀❀❀❀

Boys really are infuriating and dim, especially Year Six boys.

And Year Eight boys are not much better. Lawrie Marshall has edged his way to the front of the crowd and is reading my panda leaflet with a sneery, disgusted look on his face.

Lawrie is the scratchiest, surliest boy I've ever met. He's a loner, radiating waves of simmering anger that keep both kids and teachers at arm's length. If he were a chocolate truffle, he'd be one of Paddy's disastrous experiments – dark chocolate filled with gherkins and liquorice, or something equally horrific.

He must have a sweet tooth, though, because he always turns up at my cake sales.

'How come you think you can change the world with cake?' he snarls, bundling four cupcakes into a paper bag and handing over a pound coin.

'I just do,' I say. 'I care about the pandas, and anything I can do to raise awareness and raise money has got to help.'

'Huh,' Lawrie says. 'What's the black and white icing supposed to be, anyway? Badgers?'

❀❀❀❀❀❀❀❀❀❀❀❀❀❀❀❀❀❀❀❀❀❀❀❀

'Panda faces,' I say through gritted teeth. 'Obviously.'

'Right,' he grunts. 'Don't give up the day job, OK?'

I roll my eyes.

'Like the hat,' Lawrie sneers, stalking away. I resist the temptation to throw a rock bun at the back of his head – but only just.

'Ignore him,' Sarah says. 'He has a chip on his shoulder.'

'A what?'

'You know,' she shrugs. 'It's just one of those things that people say. He's angry at the world. Snippy with everyone. Don't take it personally.'

The teachers drift over, buying the last few cakes for the staffroom, and I hand out the remaining leaflets to anyone who will take one.

'There has to be twenty quid in there, at least,' Sarah says, grinning at the collection tin, and suddenly I feel doubtful, disappointed. Twenty quid isn't a whole lot really, especially considering all the flour and eggs and sugar and food colouring I've forked out for to make my cupcakes. It's not enough to save the giant panda, I am pretty sure. Looking around the table, I notice half a dozen discarded panda leaflets lying on the ground, and my spirits dip still further.

Saving the world with cake may actually be harder than I thought.

I glare at Lawrie Marshall as he stomps away along the corridor. I don't think he has a chip on his shoulder so much as a whole plateful of the things, drenched in vinegar.

3

Once we've counted it up properly it turns out that we have made almost £30 from the cake sale, so my mood has recovered a little by the time the last bell rings. When I get home, I will ask Mum to make a cheque out to the panda charity, and it will make a difference, I know it will. I expect £30 could plant a whole load of bamboo.

There's a steady drizzle falling as I walk down to the bus stop, but when I reach into my rucksack for my panda hat it isn't there. Maybe I left it in my locker? Once I get off the school bus in Kitnor, it's quite a long walk up to Tanglewood, and without my hat I will get wet.

'I'm going to run back and get my hat,' I tell Sarah. She lives in town, so she walks home, and at my words she just pulls up her jacket hood and shrugs.

'See you then!' she says.

I am sprinting back up to the school, dodging the crowds of kids going the other way, when I catch sight of something very odd fluttering from the school flagpole in the breeze.

My panda hat! I am outraged. Who would do such a thing?

I frown as a memory surfaces.

'Like the panda hat,' Lawrie Marshall had said at breaktime. And what he meant was that he *didn't* like the panda hat – the curl of his lip and the tone of his voice made that very clear.

I don't think he likes me and I definitely do not like him, but still, he wouldn't do something like this – would he? He seems too gloomy, too sour – I am not sure that practical jokes are his style. Then again, he sits right across the aisle from me in science, and if the hat had been at the top of my rucksack he could have swiped it easily.

I take a deep breath and storm across to the flagpole.

It takes forever to work out how to control the lines that hoist things up and down, and by then my hair is

15

frizzy from the rain and I am very cross indeed. Eventually I manage to haul down the hat and untie it, and even though it is dripping wet I pull it on because at least that way I won't lose it again.

Seriously, if I find out that Lawrie Marshall is responsible for this I will make sure he is an endangered species himself. I leg it across the grass towards the bus stop, but as I run through the playground I have a bad feeling, a very bad feeling. It is too quiet, too empty. There are no clumps of kids, no waiting school buses, just a few stray students hurrying away, umbrellas angled against the rain. I must have been messing around with that stupid flagpole for longer than I thought because I've gone and missed the bus.

Great.

I slow to a walk. Once upon a time Skye and Summer would have made sure the bus waited for me, but they are at the high school now. My friends from junior school, Amy and Jayde, usually save me a seat, but I can't blame them for not getting the driver to hang on – they probably thought I was doing something after school.

✿✿✿✿✿✿✿✿✿✿✿✿✿✿✿✿✿✿✿✿✿✿✿✿✿

I have riding lessons on Fridays, at the stables on the edge of town, and on Tuesdays I have Save the Animals Club, which I invented and which usually consists of me, Sarah, Amy and Jayde talking about pandas/whales/tigers to assorted Year Five and Six kids. Lately, our numbers have dwindled and the week before half-term even Sarah made an excuse not to come, so it was just me, sitting alone in the science room after 3.30, looking at my home-made endangered species leaflets and wondering if I was the only one who actually cared. Sometimes I skip the school bus anyway, and walk up to meet Skye, Summer and Cherry at the high school, and we go into town and drink smoothies and mooch around the shops and catch the town bus home at half five.

It looks like I'll be catching that bus today. I trudge out of the school gates and turn the corner, my panda hat dripping, and walk right into a nightmare.

Lawrie Marshall is in the shady walkway next to the school gym. He is locked in battle with a small, scrawny kid, holding him by the jacket, shaking him, growling something angry right into his face.

❀❀❀❀❀❀❀❀❀❀❀❀❀❀❀❀❀❀❀❀❀❀❀❀❀❀

The kid looks terrified, his eyes wide with fear, and I recognize the weaselly Year Six kid from earlier, the one who thought that pandas should branch out a bit and eat Big Macs and chocolate fridge cake.

My heart thuds. I hate bullying of any kind, and this is not name-calling or teasing, it is full-on aggression. Lawrie shoves the little kid up against the gym wall, and the kid winces. He wriggles helplessly, trying to get away, but Lawrie is two years older, six inches taller and a whole lot angrier. The little kid is going to be mincemeat.

'Let him go!' I scream, and two pairs of startled eyes swivel to look at me.

'Push off, panda girl,' Lawrie snarls. 'This is none of your business!'

That does it. I think of my hat, fluttering from the flagpole, a dozen nasty, snide remarks Lawrie Marshall has made in the year since he joined our school. I look at the Year Six kid, squirming as he struggles, and I see red.

I fling myself at Lawrie Marshall, grabbing his arms, pulling him backwards, away from the boy. His victim slithers free, grabs his abandoned sports bag and sprints off along the walkway, and Lawrie Marshall rounds on me, his face dark with fury.

'You idiot!' he yells. 'Now look what you've done!'

'Idiot? Me?' I yell back at him. 'You should be ashamed of yourself! You're loads bigger than that little kid, and old enough to know better . . . bullying sucks! Only losers have to threaten those who are weaker than themselves to feel good. D'you think it makes you tough? D'you think it makes you hard? It doesn't, it just makes you a lousy, rotten bully!'

Lawrie Marshall looks disgusted. His lip curls, his eyes flash and his nostrils flare dangerously. His fists are clenched and trembling, as if fighting the urge to lash out at me. Suddenly I'm scared, aware that I have just broken up a fight, yelled at a bully, shouted insults at the school misfit. Here I am on a shady walkway tucked away from the road with a psychopathic schoolboy, and trust me, he is not happy.

'Idiot,' he says again, his voice thick with scorn. 'You really think you're something, don't you? You reckon you can save the world, rescue the panda and wipe out bullying all in one day, then go home and eat your stupid little

❀❀❀❀❀❀❀❀❀❀❀❀❀❀❀❀❀❀❀❀❀❀❀❀

cakes. You don't have a clue about the real world! You don't know what you're talking about!'

Lawrie Marshall strides away, leaving me alone in the rain.

4

I spot the scrawny Year Six kid in the school corridor on Friday and corner him, concerned. 'Are you OK?' I ask. 'He hasn't bothered you again, has he?'

'Er . . . no,' the boy says shiftily. 'And yes, thanks, I'm fine. No hassle. No worries.'

His friends hover nearby, smirking. I can sense that the kid just wants to escape, but I grab his sleeve and haul him back and he rolls his eyes and tells his mates he'll catch up with them. You'd think he might be at least a little bit grateful that I saved him from being mashed to a pulp, but I guess that's boys for you.

'Have you told the teachers?' I push. 'Bullying is out of order, you know. Only lowlifes and losers pick on little kids. If that creep can do it to you, he can do it to others too, so speaking out really is the only way to stop it. Do you want me to say something to your guidance tutor?'

'No!' the kid gulps. 'No, honestly, don't say anything, I don't want a fuss . . . I've sorted it now. It won't happen again, I'm pretty sure of that. But thanks for looking out for me the other day. You saved my skin, and I appreciate that.'

I smile. 'Well . . . as long as you're sure everything's OK now?'

'I'm sure,' he says. 'And . . . look . . . I'm sorry about the hat.'

He races off along the corridor like a mad thing, bashing into a couple of Year Fives as he goes.

Boys. I will never understand them. And what did he mean about my hat?

'That was the kid Lawrie Marshall had a hold of the other day?' Sarah enquires.

'Yup. Poor thing.'

Sarah frowns. 'He doesn't look like a victim,' she says. 'More of a troublemaker. And what did he mean about your hat? Perhaps he hoisted it up the flagpole!'

'No, that had to be Lawrie,' I frown. 'He hates me,

✿✿✿✿✿✿✿✿✿✿✿✿✿✿✿✿✿✿✿✿✿✿✿✿✿✿✿

and he hates the hat. And he sits across from me in science, so . . .'

'So what?' Sarah shrugs. 'That proves nothing. You could have dropped the hat, or the Year Six kid could have taken it out of your locker . . .'

'Nah, I don't think so,' I frown. 'But whoever pulled the stunt with my hat, it doesn't change things. Lawrie Marshall is a bully, pure and simple.'

'He's definitely a loner,' Sarah says. 'He never seems to have any friends around. Maybe that's because of his temper?'

'Probably,' I agree.

'He'd be quite nice-looking if he ever smiled,' Sarah considers. 'In theory, of course. He never DOES smile – he is the sulkiest boy I know.'

'He never smiles because he is a horrible, bad-tempered bully,' I say. 'You should have seen him the other day, Sarah, it was horrible! He practically had that little kid by the throat!'

'Maybe the kid deserved it?' Sarah suggests.

'Nobody deserves that. Trust me, Lawrie Marshall is bad news.'

23

❀❀❀❀❀❀❀❀❀❀❀❀❀❀❀❀❀❀❀❀❀❀❀❀

As I finish speaking, the boy in question appears in the distance and stalks along the corridor towards us. As usual, he treats me to his best glare.

'Idiot!' he snarls as he passes.

My eyes widen in shock and my cheeks burn with embarrassment as I try to dredge up a reply.

'Oh boy.' Sarah blinks. 'I see what you mean!'

'Loser,' I mutter, but it's too little, too late, of course. Lawrie Marshall has long gone.

I am out of sorts all day after that, but I have a riding lesson after school and that is the one thing that is pretty much guaranteed to put the smile back on my face. My lesson isn't until four, so I have lots of time to walk down to the stables on the edge of town. With every step the day's irritations loosen and lift away.

I have been learning to ride since Christmas, and although I know I still have a lot to learn, I love it. I love the smell of the stable yard, all fresh hay and ponies and leather. I love the paddock exercises my instructor teaches us for balance and confidence, scissors and frogs and round-the-world turns and riding with no stirrups. I love hacking through the countryside or riding along the beach, trotting or cantering with the wind in my face and the feeling that I'm free, soaring, that anything at all is possible.

Most of all, though, I love a pony called Caramel.

I liked her first of all because of her name – caramel, as you know, is my favourite sweet treat. Then I fell for her looks because Caramel is possibly the most beautiful pony in the world. She is a pure-bred Exmoor pony, twelve hands high and a beautiful dark bay colour, rich as caramel. Around her eyes and muzzle are pangaré markings, mealy-cream, and her mane and tail are thick and coarse and wild. She looks timeless, noble, magical, as though she could have ridden out of the Dark Ages, been the pony of a princess warrior or a Celtic queen from thousands of years ago.

She is my perfect pony, but I have never ridden her because unlike most Exmoors, who are steady and calm and trustworthy, Caramel can be hard to handle. The bosses at the riding school, Jean and Roy, think she was ill-treated in the past – she can be jumpy, unpredictable, flighty. There have been a couple of unpleasant incidents with Caramel this year, and Jean and Roy are wary. They

✿✿✿✿✿✿✿✿✿✿✿✿✿✿✿✿✿✿✿✿✿✿✿✿✿✿✿

make sure that only older, more experienced riders take her out these days.

It's the story of my life – everybody thinks I am too young for everything. They don't take me seriously at all.

For example, a couple of weeks ago there was a part-time job advertised at the stables for someone to help with mucking out and grooming, just a few hours for a couple of days a week after school. When Mum picked me up after my lesson that day, I was full of it – how I could spend more time with Caramel, get more experience with horses, cover the cost of my lessons and bring a little cash in on top of that. I thought she'd go for the idea for sure, but I was wrong.

Surprise, surprise, she said I was too young.

'You're only twelve,' she'd said on the drive home, as if I might have forgotten this vital fact. 'They probably wouldn't consider you for the job at that age, and besides, there's no need to start thinking about part-time jobs just yet! Just focus on your friends and your animals and your studies!'

'But . . .'

'No buts,' Mum insisted. 'Don't be in too much of a

❀❀❀❀❀❀❀❀❀❀❀❀❀❀❀❀❀❀❀❀❀❀❀❀

hurry to grow up, Coco. Enjoy your freedom while you can! If it's the money you're thinking about, I'll have a word with Paddy – now that the chocolate business is starting to take off, we might be able to give you a bit more pocket money.'

Pocket money? Honestly, I felt about five years old. As far as my family is concerned I might as well be – it's as if there is one rule for my sisters and another for me.

OK, I'm twelve. So what? At twelve Summer had been a regular student helper at the dance school for years. By the time she was thirteen she worked a whole week there in the summer holidays in exchange for extra lessons, and Skye was thirteen when she helped out with the costumes on the TV film they made in Kitnor a few months back. The twins aren't all that much older than me, but they get to do what they want.

As for Honey, she may not have had a job at twelve but she had way more freedom than any of us. She was a pre-teen drama queen – she didn't bother to ask permission for the things she wanted to do, she just went ahead and did them anyway. She still does. Maybe I should take a leaf out of her book?

27

❀❀❀❀❀❀❀❀❀❀❀❀❀❀❀❀❀❀❀❀❀❀❀❀

I push through the gates of the Woodlands Riding School, breathing in the smell of fresh hay and happiness. I am a little early, but I like it that way. I wave at Kelly, one of the teenage instructors who sometimes takes the paddock classes or leads the treks, then step into the warm office building, stash my rucksack in a locker and nip to the loos to change into my riding gear. Folding away my school uniform and replacing it with outsize jumper, jodhpurs and waterproof, I am the happiest I have felt all day. I leave my uniform in the locker and scoop up my riding hat, pulling it on as I wander back out into the stable yard.

Then I see a familiar figure in the doorway of one stall, gruff and grim in wellies and muddy jeans, forking manure into a wheelbarrow.

Lawrie Marshall looks up at me and his face registers surprise and then disgust. I am pretty sure my face mirrors those emotions too, and then some.

5

'What are you doing here?' Lawrie Marshall asks, and I swear I am so cross at this comment that if I could I would tip that barrowload of manure right over his head, then jab him with his own pitchfork, just for good measure.

'I am here for my riding lesson,' I tell him. 'The same as I have been every week since January. And I have never seen you at Woodlands before, so I think I could ask what *you* are doing here!'

Lawrie curls his lip. 'I work here,' he says icily. 'Started this week, three forty-five till six, Tuesdays and Fridays. If I'd known they gave lessons to fruitcakes like you, I might have had second thoughts . . .'

Fruitcake? Me? I am pretty sure this is an insult and not a reference to my baking abilities. And worse, it looks

❁❁❁❁❁❁❁❁❁❁❁❁❁❁❁❁❁❁❁❁❁❁❁

like Lawrie Marshall has *my* job. He is the same age as me, twelve years old . . . is that fair? Is that right? No, it is not.

'Oh . . . fruitcake to you too!' I snap.

As comebacks go, it isn't the best. You might even say it is lame and laughable, and Lawrie seems to think so because his lips twitch into a sour kind of smile and he starts shovelling manure again, a little carelessly. A clump of something deeply unpleasant lands sloppily on my boots, and I am pretty certain it wasn't an accident.

Words fail me. I turn on my heel and march over to Caramel's stall, seething inwardly. I reach up and stroke her face, press my cheek against the roughness of her through-a-hedge-backwards mane, inhaling her smell which is like dust and hay and sweet molasses all mixed up together.

'I do not like that boy,' I whisper so that only Caramel can hear. 'I do not like him at all.' She nuzzles me gently and I slide my arms around her neck, letting my anger dissolve. A few minutes later I am smiling again, feeding Caramel slices of apple from my palm.

'She likes you,' Kelly says, behind me. 'Caramel. You're

good with her, Coco . . . not many people are. Come on, let's get you saddled up. Jean and Roy aren't here today, so I thought we'd do some exercises in the paddock . . . who would you like to ride, Bailey or Jojo?'

I frown. I like Bailey and I like Jojo, but the pony I most want to ride is Caramel. I am pretty certain she would behave well for me. She likes me – even Kelly can see that. And Jean and Roy are not here today, so maybe we can bend the rules a little?

'Can't I ride Caramel?' I plead. 'Jean said I was getting much better, much more confident. She said I would be ready to take Caramel out . . .'

She did say this, but she didn't specify when. I have the feeling the date Jean had in mind was several years ahead, but Kelly doesn't need to know this.

'I don't think so,' Kelly frowns. 'Not today. Caramel can be pretty tricky. Jean and Roy aren't even sure she's the right kind of pony for us – a riding school horse has to earn its keep, and Caramel can be unpredictable . . .'

I bite my lip. This doesn't sound good. If Jean and Roy aren't sure about the little Exmoor pony, she may be coming to the end of her time at the Woodlands

❀❀❀❀❀❀❀❀❀❀❀❀❀❀❀❀❀❀❀❀❀❀❀❀

Riding School. Unless I can prove once and for all that she can behave well?

'Jean said I could!' I argue, aware that I am stretching the truth more than a little. 'She says I have a connection with Caramel, that I'm a natural with her! Please let me try, Kelly? It's only in the paddock. What could go wrong?'

'Plenty,' Kelly says, but I can tell that she's weakening. 'Maybe if Jean was here . . .'

'She isn't, though!' I sigh. 'Please, Kelly? I've been looking forward to this all week!'

Kelly rolls her eyes. 'Oh, go on then,' she says. 'But if it all goes pear-shaped . . .'

'It won't!' I grin.

'Lawrie?' she yells across the yard. 'Can you get Caramel saddled up, please? For Coco here.'

Lawrie raises an eyebrow. 'I thought you said only experienced riders could take Caramel?' he questions, and I can tell Kelly feels hassled by the comment. Now that the decision is made, she doesn't want to go back on it.

'Jean said it would be OK,' she tells Lawrie, walking

away to help the other students get mounted. There are six of us today, but the other five are younger than me and need more support. They wait patiently as Kelly matches them with their ponies.

'I am an experienced rider, you know,' I say, as Lawrie saddles up Caramel and adjusts the stirrups. 'I know what I'm doing.'

'I doubt that somehow,' Lawrie says. 'Caramel is easily scared, OK? Go easy with her.'

'She likes me!'

'That makes one of us, I suppose,' he mutters, leading the pony out into the yard and holding her while I climb on. Luckily, Caramel stands as quiet and still as a mouse and I manage it smoothly. I collect the reins and press my heels gently into the pony's sides, and we walk forward across the yard to join Kelly and the other kids.

Caramel really does like me, I can tell. She seems calm and steady and settled as we walk down to the paddock and circle round, and when Kelly asks us to follow a figure-of-eight pattern and then negotiate a basic obstacle course, she takes it all in her stride. Nobody would ever guess she was a 'problem' pony.

33

Kelly looks less anxious now, more confident. She has taken a risk letting me ride Caramel – I am not about to let her down. I plan to show her that I am a good rider, and more than that, that Caramel really can be trusted. All she needs is to be treated gently.

'Rising trot,' Kelly calls out, and I ease the pony forward smoothly. She trots beautifully, and when Kelly suggests that three of us try a canter, I know she is really starting to trust me. Caramel speeds up and I lean forward, exhilarated, enjoying every moment. This is without a doubt the best riding lesson I've ever had – it's as though the pony is a part of me, or I am part of her. We understand each other, and I know that she is loving this as much as I am.

Maybe Caramel was born of feral stock, the ponies living wild on the moors; maybe she was treated roughly at some point in her past; maybe, but I know she trusts me and I know she has it in her to be the best pony ever.

'Excellent, Coco!' Kelly calls as we slow to a walk again, and I can feel myself glowing with pride. 'Great, all of you. Right, folks, we'll cool down with some control

❀❀❀❀❀❀❀❀❀❀❀❀❀❀❀❀❀❀❀❀❀❀

exercises. Let's start off with "Round the World". If you're not sure, kids, watch Coco, she does this one really well . . .'

My cheeks glow pink with pleasure at the compliment, but I've been doing the paddock exercises for ages now, and I know I am good at them. 'Round the World' is all about teaching the rider balance and control – you have to scissor one leg over the pony's neck, so that you are balanced sideways on the saddle; then scissor again until you are sitting backwards in the saddle; again so that you are riding sideways to the other side; and once more until you are finally facing front again.

This exercise is always a little chaotic, with riders slipping and slithering about in a very undignified way, but I have it down to a fine art. To start with, you do it while your pony is standing still, then work up to doing it on the move. I am pretty good at both. I squeeze my heels gently inwards so that Caramel walks forward, then slide my feet out of the stirrups. Aware of the younger kids watching me, I shift my balance and scissor my leg up over Caramel's neck and down again.

My leg is still hovering in mid-air when the pony lurches

✿✿✿✿✿✿✿✿✿✿✿✿✿✿✿✿✿✿✿✿✿✿✿✿

forward into a sprint, then jolts to an abrupt stop. Caramel rears up, whinnying, and suddenly I am flying through the air. There's a thump as I land in a heap on the grass, my head hitting the edge of one of the obstacle course markers, my jaw hitting the gravel path. For a moment, I am seeing stars.

'Coco?' Kelly is saying, on her knees beside me. 'Coco, are you all right?'

I try to sit up and fall back again instantly. My head feels like it has been sliced open with an axe.

'*Ouchheee . . .*'

Kelly stands up and yells at the top of her voice for the first-aid kit, and I scrunch my eyes tightly closed and wish the ground would open up and swallow me. It doesn't, of course, and even with my eyes closed I know that five little kids watched my fall from grace with shock and horror. Oh, the shame of it . . .

Caramel, how could you do this to me? I thought we had an understanding . . .

A damp cloth smelling of witch hazel is pressed to my chin and my eyes snap open abruptly.

'There, that should help,' Kelly says, and over her

36

shoulder I see Lawrie Marshall with the first-aid box and the witch hazel, his face dark and disapproving.

I think I will survive the bump, but the wound to my pride may be fatal. This is the most humiliating moment of my life.

6

Sadly, it is not just my pride that has taken a battering. It would have been a lot worse without the riding hat, but still, there is a purple-red graze along my jaw and a whole constellation of bruises all over my bum and legs. Great.

'What did you *do*?' Skye demands as I hobble into the kitchen at Tanglewood, the cloth soaked in witch hazel pressed to my jaw. 'You look awful!'

'Thanks,' I sigh. 'You're a real comfort, Skye. I had an argument with my favourite pony . . . she got tired of behaving beautifully and decided to throw me off.'

'Seriously?' Summer chimes in. 'She threw you? What kind of psycho horses do they have at that place? It's supposed to be a riding school, not a rodeo!'

'Don't,' I say. 'It's taken me the whole drive home to convince Mum not to make a complaint.'

'I didn't want to complain, exactly,' Mum sighs. 'I just wanted to say . . . well, that pony really shouldn't be part of a riding school. She's too high-spirited, too nervy!'

'Mum,' I argue, 'I told you – it was all my own fault.'

'How come?' Cherry demands.

A dark blush seeps across my cheeks. I don't want to come clean, but if Caramel's future is in question I can't stay quiet.

'I didn't have permission to ride Caramel,' I admit. 'She's a bit unpredictable. Hard to handle. Jean and Roy only let the really confident riders take her out, but she's my favourite pony and they were away today. So I managed to convince one of the assistants to let me ride Caramel . . . I kind of pretended I'd been told I could.'

'But you hadn't,' Skye says. 'Boy, will you be in trouble!'

'I don't expect Jean and Roy will be impressed,' Mum comments, making teas and hot chocolates all round.

'Well, I agree with Mum,' Summer frowns. 'This Caramel doesn't sound like the kind of horse that should be around kids at all. She sounds dangerous.'

I put a hand to my aching head. Suppose Jean and Roy think that too? I wanted to help Caramel, but maybe I've made things worse for her. Whatever my sisters think, I know that Caramel did everything perfectly. It was only when I started shifting about that she lost the plot . . . she freaked out when I scissored my leg up over her neck. Maybe she doesn't like unexpected things, or things she can't see properly. Perhaps she thought I was going to hurt her?

If I could find out what was happening the other times she's behaved badly, maybe I could work out what's upsetting her and solve the problem, and then surely Jean and Roy won't even think about getting rid of her.

'Good job you had your hard hat on, baby sister,' Summer grins. 'You might have done some real damage!'

'I am not a baby,' I scowl. 'C'mon, you're only seventeen months older than me!'

'Maybe, but you'll always be the baby of the family to us,' Skye teases. 'We worry about you!'

'Well, don't!' I huff. 'I am very grown-up and independent, and you know it!'

'Now, now,' Mum says. 'Don't tease your sister, girls!'

40

❀❀❀❀❀❀❀❀❀❀❀❀❀❀❀❀❀❀❀❀❀❀

That makes me feel like a three-year-old in the middle of a squabble.

Mum sets down hot drinks and a plate of home-baked chocolate chip cookies, scooping up a couple along with a mug of tea to take out to the workshop because Paddy is working late on a special sample order for some big department store. It has to be finished and sent off by Special Delivery to arrive on Monday, but apparently it will be worth all the hard work and long hours if they land the contract.

As soon as Mum has gone, Skye leans forward. 'It's not *you* I'm worrying about really, Coco,' she says in a whisper. 'It's Honey. I honestly thought she was trying harder after the mix-up at the start of term when we thought she'd gone missing, and all that stirring it with Shay. Well, it doesn't look like it. My art teacher asked me today when Honey would be back at school – she must have been skipping lessons. The teachers seem to think she's ill, so maybe she's sent in a forged note or something?'

'No way!' I gasp.

'She gets the school bus with us every day, the same as

always,' Cherry says. 'None of us had a clue she was skiving!'

'She may be on the bus, but she obviously isn't making it past the gates,' Skye shrugs. 'I know she likes to hang around by the wall at the front before the bell goes, but it looks like that's as far as she's getting. Wait till Mum finds out – she'll go nuts!'

'She will,' Summer says softly. 'Mum has enough on her plate already, with the B&B and the chocolate business and . . . well, stuff.'

Nobody comments, but we all know that Summer's illness is the part of the 'stuff' that is bothering Mum just now. A few months back, Summer put herself under so much pressure to succeed she just about unravelled in the process. For a while it seemed like she was trying to starve herself, and now she has to go to twice-weekly meetings at an eating-disorders clinic at the hospital in Exeter.

She had to give up her dance school place and watch her friend Jodie take it instead. Summer still goes to ballet class in Minehead, but she must think about the scholarship place she let slip through her fingers. We don't really

❀❀❀❀❀❀❀❀❀❀❀❀❀❀❀❀❀❀❀❀❀❀❀❀

talk about that and we don't mention her eating disorder either – we just tiptoe around her, scared to upset her, scared to say something that might make her feel bad. Although she has put a little weight back on, Summer is still fragile, brittle, with pale skin and blue shadows beneath her beautiful eyes. You get the feeling that if you held her too hard she might snap, crumble.

Mum says that time is a great healer, that we need to be patient and positive and kind, but I know that she worries about Summer – we all do. The last thing any of us needs is for Honey to go off the rails again on top of that.

Summer frowns. 'It's like Honey just can't help it, you know? She tries to get her act together, but she can't keep it up . . .'

I think that Honey can help it, actually. Ever since Dad left a few years ago, my big sister has been lurching from one disaster to the next. It's kind of exhausting to live with, and these days my patience is wearing thin.

'D'you think we should keep quiet about this?' Skye asks. 'Pretend we don't know? Or . . . should we tell? Not to get Honey into trouble, obviously, but . . . well, to stop

✿✿✿✿✿✿✿✿✿✿✿✿✿✿✿✿✿✿✿✿✿✿✿✿✿✿✿✿

her from getting into more trouble than she is in already, if that makes sense?'

'We can't,' Summer says. 'Sisters stick together, right?'

I bite my lip. The family rule that we don't tell tales is unshakeable, but I can't help wishing someone would speak out about Honey. It's no fun watching your big sister mess her life up.

'Maybe we should tell?' I venture.

'But . . . she'd never forgive us,' Summer points out.

There's a silence as we think about the fallout if we did dare tell. More than once, Mum has threatened Honey with boarding school, and this could just be the last straw. None of us wants to be responsible for that.

'The high school reports are out next Wednesday,' Cherry says. 'I guess Charlotte will find out then. No use stirring things up when we know it's going to come out anyway, right?'

'Right,' we agree.

The kitchen door swings open and Mum comes in again with an empty tray, humming some old tune from the Dark Ages. 'Nobody hungry?' she asks, scanning the untouched plate of cookies. 'That makes a change!'

❀❀❀❀❀❀❀❀❀❀❀❀❀❀❀❀❀❀❀❀❀❀

We all reach for the biscuits and bite into them guiltily, except for Summer who just breaks hers in half and feeds fragments slowly to Fred the dog.

Let's just say I am not looking forward to Wednesday.

7

By the time Wednesday rolls around my graze is healing, but the bruises on my legs have mellowed to rainbow shades of blue, purple and greenish-yellow. They look especially attractive with my gym shorts, and I have to recount the story of how the unpredictable, half-wild Exmoor pony at Woodlands got startled by something and threw me off.

'You have to get used to these things when you move on to riding more challenging horses,' I say. 'But they're the most rewarding ones, of course . . .'

I am not sure how many of my friends totally believe this version of events, but they say nothing.

I have been trying to steer clear of Lawrie Marshall. He wasn't in science on Monday – there was a football

❀❀❀❀❀❀❀❀❀❀❀❀❀❀❀❀❀❀❀❀❀❀❀❀

match apparently – but we have science again last lesson today and I am not looking forward to that. Should I blank him? Or smile sweetly and thank him for his help on Friday in the hope that he chokes on his own self-righteousness? He was as grumpy as ever when he handed over the first-aid kit, but while I was getting my bearings again I watched him catch Caramel and calm and coax her back up to the stable yard. Lawrie Marshall has zero charm with human beings, but I have to admit he's good with horses.

I have almost decided to swallow my pride and let bygones be bygones when Lawrie walks into class, throws his bag down across the aisle and shoots me the kind of look that could curdle milk.

'Pleased with yourself, are you?' he says coldly.

'Pleased?' I frown. 'What d'you mean?'

'You don't even know?' he asks, shaking his head slowly. 'You don't even care?'

'About what?' I frown, but Lawrie Marshall just glares and turns his back on me. Mr Harper starts the lesson and I have to sit there for fifty whole minutes gritting my teeth and wondering why I ever thought that saying thank you to the Year Eight bully was a good plan. He is sourer than stewed rhubarb without the sugar, bitter as aspirin.

What a loser. How come he always manages to make *me* feel like I'm the one who's done something wrong?

His comments get under my skin and bug me all lesson, and by the time the bell goes I decide to confront him. I tell Sarah I want to talk to Mr Harper about endangered antelopes because she may be my best friend, but she has a one-track mind when it comes to boys. Lately, she is much more interested in who fancies who than the plight of the white rhino and the blue whale, and if she made some quip about me and Lawrie Marshall I would not be amused. The minute she's gone I pack my things and run; I catch up with Lawrie on the playground, and my temper boils over.

'Hey!' I yell. 'I want to talk to you!'

He turns round, raising one eyebrow. 'I don't want to talk to you, so tough luck,' he snaps.

'What is your problem?' I demand. 'No wonder you don't have any friends! No wonder everyone thinks you're weird. You're just a spiteful, horrible bully!'

Lawrie Marshall flinches as if I've slapped him.

❀❀❀❀❀❀❀❀❀❀❀❀❀❀❀❀❀❀❀❀❀❀❀

'Shut up,' he scowls. 'You don't know what you're talking about.'

'I know exactly what I'm talking about,' I tell him. 'But you – you just spout rubbish! What did you mean earlier, about me feeling pleased with myself, and not even caring?'

He shakes his head. 'You are probably the most spoilt, selfish girl I have ever met,' he says. 'You lied about being allowed to ride Caramel, didn't you?'

'No, I –'

'You lied, and it all went wrong, and Kelly was in trouble.'

'What about me?' I protest. 'I was the one who got hurt!'

'You deserved it,' he shrugs. 'And after all that, you didn't even bother to apologize or call the stables to find out what was happening.'

A flicker of unease stirs within me.

'So . . . what is happening?' I ask.

'Plenty,' he snarls. 'The stables are selling Caramel. So, yeah, like I said, I hope you're pleased with yourself. It's all your fault.'

49

✿ ✿

He turns on his heel and walks away. Me, I stand very still in the playground, letting the waves of shame and guilt slide over me.

Then the school bus toots and starts its engine, and I run down to the gates and scramble aboard, just in time.

I am still upset when I arrive home. We finish a little ahead of the high school, so I'm usually home before my sisters and I'm planning to ask Mum if we can call the stables and ask them to hang on to Caramel. It's a long shot, but it has to be worth a try. When I walk into the kitchen, though, I find Mum and Paddy dancing around with champagne glasses in their hands. Fred the dog is leaping madly round their feet, and even Humbug my pet sheep has made her way into the kitchen and is curled up on an armchair in the corner.

The sight of this is enough to put a smile back on my face, briefly at any rate.

'So this is what you get up to when we're at school then?' I tease.

'Oh, Coco, love, we're celebrating!' Mum laughs. 'You'll never guess what's happened!'

❀❀❀❀❀❀❀❀❀❀❀❀❀❀❀❀❀❀❀❀❀

'Don't tell me – your three-month wedding anniversary?' I suggest. 'A lottery win?'

'As good as,' Paddy says in his cool Glaswegian accent. 'We've only gone and landed a major order from the Miller-Brown chain of department stores! They received my samples on Monday, and they really loved them. They've offered us the chance to supply fifty of their top stores with the option to expand into all of them if our chocolates do well . . .'

'And they will do well,' Mum laughs, taking another champagne glass from the cupboard, filling it up with pink lemonade from the fridge and handing it to me. 'They will do brilliantly because they are the best truffles in the entire universe and now everyone will get the chance to know that!'

I clink my glass against theirs. 'Was my truffle in the box of samples?' I want to know. 'The one named after me?'

'Well, of course,' Paddy says. 'All the chocolates you girls have inspired were in the box. Marshmallow Skye and Summer's Dream and Cherry Crush and Coco Caramel. There's even one called Sweet Honey, although your big sister says she doesn't like chocolate . . .'

✿✿✿✿✿✿✿✿✿✿✿✿✿✿✿✿✿✿✿✿✿✿✿✿

I'm not so sure about that. My big sister likes chocolate all right, she just doesn't like Paddy.

'The buyers at Miller-Brown loved them, though,' he continues. 'The whole concept – the taste, the names, the packaging, the fair-trade angle . . . all of it. This order is *big*. It could take us off the breadline and into profit! It's epic!'

I blink. I wonder just how much profit a big order like that could bring in? The seed of an idea forms in my mind, growing quickly.

Caramel is for sale. Well, OK, that's my fault, kind of – but maybe, just maybe, if we could actually buy her, the story might still have a happy ending. It's not such a crazy thought, surely?

The possibilities bubble up inside me, sweeter than pink lemonade.

ATTENDANCE * RECORD *
EXMOOR HIGH SCHOOL
Honey Tanberry..............100%

Parents
Honey T

8

I bite my lip. 'Are we going to be rich?' I ask. 'Will we have lots of money?'

'Rich? Well, I wouldn't go that far,' Paddy says. 'We should be able to pay off our business loans, at any rate.'

Ah. Business loans. I had forgotten about them.

'We might just have enough to stretch as far as a takeaway curry,' Mum teases. 'By way of celebration. And perhaps we can let the B&B run down a little and turn Tanglewood back into a real family home.'

'Right,' I check. 'That's great. But . . . not enough to buy a pony, say?'

'A pony?'

'Mum, the stables are selling Caramel!' I explain. 'It's all my fault, and I thought that if we could just buy her . . .'

Mum holds her hands up. 'Whoa, whoa, a minute,' she says. 'Three things, Coco. First of all, if that pony is sold on it won't be your fault – she was clearly not suited to be a riding school horse. Second, no, I'm really sorry, but we won't have that kind of money – we don't have any money yet; we have to send the orders out first! Third . . . well, if we did have the cash to buy a pony, I certainly wouldn't choose Caramel. She's already thrown you once. I don't think she's trustworthy!'

'She is!' I wail. 'She is the best pony in the whole world, and if we could just save her . . . Mum, I want this more than anything! It could be all my birthday and Christmas presents from now right up until I die, I swear! Please!'

'Coco, listen –'

'Will you think about it? Please?' I beg. 'Just consider it? Maybe we could pay Jean and Roy in instalments? You know I've always wanted a pony, and I love Caramel, I really do! I will never, ever ask for anything again, truly.'

A look passes between Mum and Paddy, a quiet, thoughtful look that sets my heart racing. Maybe they really will consider it?

'We'll talk about it later,' Mum says. 'It's a huge

❀❀❀❀❀❀❀❀❀❀❀❀❀❀❀❀❀❀❀❀❀❀❀❀

decision, and there are all kinds of reasons why now is not the right time for it, and really, you know yourself that Caramel is not the kind of pony I'd choose. So we'll think about it, yes; we'll talk about it; but that's all. Don't get your hopes up, Coco, I am not promising anything.'

I grin. 'Thank you, Mum!' I whoop. 'Thank you, Paddy!'

I clink glasses with them again, cranking up the volume on Mum's iPod, so happy I think I might burst. OK, Mum hasn't said yes . . . but she hasn't said no either. All is not lost!

Mum starts to dance again, taking me by the hand and dragging me up as well. The three of us are strutting our stuff to Abba's 'Dancing Queen' when Cherry, Summer, Skye and Honey come in from school. Their faces are serious, and they are all clutching big brown envelopes.

I remember what Cherry said about the high school reports being out today, and I have a strong feeling that the happy mood is about to crash.

Mum and Paddy launch into the story of the big order again, pouring more pink lemonade, failing to notice the serious faces. My sisters go along with it all, asking about the order, congratulating Paddy, talking of fame and fortune and chocolate-flavoured world domination.

Only Honey is silent. She waits for as long as she can bear, then flings her report down on the tabletop as if throwing down a challenge.

'Look,' she says. 'Better get it over with. It's report day – I mean, I know it won't be good, but I have been trying a lot harder, so . . .'

Mum and Paddy are serious suddenly, sitting down at the table, slicing open the envelope. Skye is chewing her lip, Summer is studying the ceiling and Cherry looks like she'd rather be anywhere, anywhere at all, than here.

Honey seems more relaxed than any of us, perched on the kitchen table, helping herself to an apple from the fruit dish as if she hasn't a care in the world. I can't help admiring her confidence.

To be honest, I am a little surprised she has shown her face at all because she must know exactly what's in that school report. Perhaps it's like she says, and she just wants to get the whole thing over with?

Mum frowns as she scans the first page, leafing through,

studying each sheet in turn. Paddy is reading too, and finally, after the longest few minutes in the history of the world, Mum shakes her head and puts the report booklet down.

'Well . . . what can I say?'

'Is it OK?' Honey asks, still crunching apple. 'Have I improved?' Her jaw-length blonde hair falls across her face and her eyes look anxious, hopeful.

Mum laughs. 'Honey, it's more than OK,' she says. 'It's . . . well, it's an excellent report! The best report you've brought home since primary school. Well done! I am so pleased – I knew you could do it!'

Skye catches my gaze, a flicker of confusion in her eyes. Something doesn't feel quite right here.

'*Much improved attitude,*' Paddy reads out. '*Working hard to make up for lost time; bright, helpful, a pleasure to have in class* . . . this is terrific, Honey!'

My big sister shrugs and slides off the tabletop. 'Well, that's me off the hook then,' she laughs. 'How about you guys? Time to face the music?'

As Skye, Summer and Cherry hand over their school reports, I cannot help myself – I lean across and look at

❀❀❀❀❀❀❀❀❀❀❀❀❀❀❀❀❀❀❀❀❀❀

the top page of Honey's report because I seriously don't believe what I am hearing.

And there it is in black and white, printed out and signed by the school principal; *Attendance: 100 per cent.*

Skye, Summer and Cherry have all brought home reasonable reports, and mine came home before the October break and that was OK too. There is no doubt about it, though – Honey's report steals the show. My off-the-rails sister has turned model pupil overnight, just in time for her GCSE year.

'Looks like I got it wrong,' Skye whispers as I collect my violin, pull on my panda hat and slip outside to practise. 'Maybe my art teacher had Honey mixed up with someone else?'

I shrug, but personally, I cannot see how. Art is the only subject Honey actually enjoys, so the art teachers know her better than most – and let's face it, whatever else she may be, my big sister is not forgettable. Still, you cannot argue with a school report, can you?

I sit in my oak tree, leaning back against the trunk, playing jiggy tunes on my old violin. The branches are getting bare now, so I can see the blue sky darkening to velvet black. Paddy has rung down to the village for a takeaway curry feast, and everyone is hopeful because Summer said she really fancied pakoras and mango chutney, and maybe that is a sign that things are getting back to normal for her too.

Really, it's a night for celebration. A big order from a nationwide department store – that could mean real success for Mum and Paddy's business. And maybe Honey really is getting her act together and will scoop a whole bunch of A* grades at GCSE? Who knows.

I'll believe it when I see it.

All I can think about is the chance of putting things right for Caramel and actually, finally, having a pony of my own. Mum and Paddy might be talking about it right now, Mum setting the kitchen table, pouring more champagne and pink lemonade. They will want to know more about Caramel, of course. They will want to know whether she can be trained, trusted, relied upon. They will want to talk to Jean and Roy about prices and check with the farmer who owns the land next to us if we can rent one of the fields for grazing.

❀ ❀

Still, all of that could happen.

I imagine shopping for saddles and bridles and horse blankets, wonder whether Humbug the sheep will be willing to share stable space. By the time the first stars come out between the branches and the little blue van from the Bengal Rose Takeaway chugs into the driveway to deliver our celebration feast, I am fizzing with happiness, with hope.

9

I manage to steer clear of Lawrie Marshall for the rest of the week at school. OK, so he thinks I'm spoilt and selfish and to blame for Caramel being sold. So what? Why should I care what he thinks? Maybe he is upset about Caramel, but he's still a lowlife bully.

Besides, I am hopeful that Mum and Paddy will make a decision about Caramel soon. I've been nagging Mum to ring the riding stables, but she says it's not something that can be decided overnight, and that she'd need to be reassured that it would be possible to train Caramel to be calmer, less jumpy.

Still, the fact that she is actually considering it is good enough for me. I plan to apologize to Jean and Roy about what happened last week, then let them know that we

❁❁❁❁❁❁❁❁❁❁❁❁❁❁❁❁❁❁❁❁❁❁❁❁❁❁

are interested in buying Caramel. Hopefully, they will talk to Mum about it when she comes to pick me up after class – once she actually meets Caramel I am pretty sure she will be as smitten as I am.

I am early as usual on Friday, and luckily there is no sign of Lawrie Marshall, although a big, shiny, silver four-wheel drive with a horsebox hitched to it is parked right across the yard. I head in towards the loos to get changed, and as I pass the office I notice a tall, sharp-faced man in a tweedy brown suit is in there talking to Jean and Roy. He looks kind of posh in a country land-owner kind of way, but there is a cold, no-nonsense look about him. He is probably some kind of country vet or a salesman selling saddles and horse blankets.

As I pass, his eyes skim over me then slide away, unimpressed.

When I emerge five minutes later to stack my rucksack and school clothes in a locker, the tweedy guy is still there. This is very annoying because I need to apologize and tell Jean and Roy that we might be able to buy Caramel, as long as they don't need to sell her in a hurry. Whatever they are talking about must be important. Still, I suppose

✿✿✿✿✿✿✿✿✿✿✿✿✿✿✿✿✿✿✿✿✿✿✿

it delays the dreaded moment of having to say sorry for pulling the wool over Kelly's eyes and trying to convince the stable's bosses that I should be Caramel's new owner. I'll have to explain after my ride.

Out in the yard, there is still no sign of Lawrie and I allow myself to wonder if he has switched his days at the stable to avoid me. Better still, maybe he's been sacked?

Kelly has saddled Bailey, a quiet strawberry roan, for me. Bailey is the slowest, stodgiest pony at Woodlands – you could send your ninety-three-year-old great-granny out for a ride on him and she'd probably complain he was too dull. Still, I know better than to argue this time as Kelly hands me the reins.

'Have you seen Lawrie?' she asks me as I swing up into the saddle.

'Sorry, no . . .'

'Oh, for goodness' sake,' Kelly frowns. 'He could at least have called in if he wasn't going to turn up for work. He seemed so keen, but . . . obviously not.'

Not sacked then. Yet.

Kelly leads out Strider, one of the bigger ponies,

❀❀❀❀❀❀❀❀❀❀❀❀❀❀❀❀❀❀❀❀❀❀❀

mounting neatly before nudging him forward so she can unhook the gate.

'Jean and Roy wanted Lawrie to bring Caramel down to the paddock, but I expect they'll manage themselves,' Kelly sighs. 'Let's go. It's just us today – the Dempsey kids have chickenpox, Jake's at the dentist and Courtney and Jenna are at a party, so . . . nice and quiet! I thought we'd take a hack through the woods.'

'I can take Caramel down to the paddock if you like,' I offer. 'I don't mind! I could fill in for Lawrie if you need me to, instead of a lesson. Or, if Lawrie's quit –'

'Not a chance,' my instructor says firmly, waiting for me to walk Bailey through the gate before closing it behind me. 'Lawrie will turn up at some point, and your mum has paid for this lesson so a lesson is what you'll get. Jean and Roy have made it clear they don't want you anywhere near Caramel – you weren't exactly truthful with me last week about being allowed to ride her, were you?'

I hang my head.

Kelly leads us down into the woods, Strider picking his way.

❀❀❀❀❀❀❀❀❀❀❀❀❀❀❀❀❀❀❀❀❀❀❀❀

'I'm sorry,' I say, falling into place behind her. 'About last week. I really didn't mean to get you into trouble – I was trying to help Caramel, show that she could be good and quiet and steady. She's my favourite pony – we have this special bond, you know? I was trying to make sure she stayed at Woodlands.'

'Things didn't quite work out then, did they?' Kelly sighs.

'Don't,' I groan. 'Caramel is up for sale, and it's all my fault!'

'Don't be too hard on yourself,' Kelly shrugs. 'It probably would have happened anyway. She's always been a "problem" pony, and there's no room for difficult horses in a riding school. Jean and Roy just can't take the risk.'

'Well, I've got a plan,' I say, reining Bailey into step alongside her. 'I've asked my mum, and guess what? I think we'll probably be buying Caramel!'

Kelly looks surprised. 'Seriously? Your mum said that?'

I bite my lip. 'Not exactly,' I hedge. 'She said she'd think about it. Possibly. Maybe . . .'

65

Kelly rolls her eyes, and in that moment she reminds me of my big sisters. I know she's laughing at me.

'Possibly?' she echoes. 'Maybe? That doesn't sound too definite!'

'It will be,' I protest as the ponies move steadily through the trees, hooves crunching down on twigs and dried leaves beneath. 'I'm working on her. I am pretty sure I can talk her round.'

'This is a pony we're talking about, Coco, not a new computer game!' Kelly says. 'You can't just nag your mum and hope she gives in. It's a huge undertaking, a real commitment.'

'I know!' I insist. 'Of course! I am a hundred per cent committed!'

Kelly looks at me, and her eyes reveal a mixture of sadness and pity and exasperation. I know what she's thinking – it's what people always think. That I'm too young, too silly; not to be taken seriously.

'I honestly don't think it'll happen,' Kelly says kindly. 'For all kinds of reasons. Caramel is a challenging pony – I know you love her, and you do have a good connection with her, but you've seen yourself how unpredictable she can be. She needs an experienced owner. Jean and Roy would never sell her to a novice rider, even if your mum really did want to buy her.'

'I'll talk to them,' I argue. 'I'll apologize, explain. I might not be the best rider in the world, but . . . Caramel deserves a home where she'll be loved. They have to give me a chance, Kelly!'

'Coco, I hate to tell you, but I think you're too late,' she says. 'It's already sorted – that bloke in the office is almost certainly going to buy her.'

A sharp pang of grief shoots through me, dulling to a sad, heavy ache. I'm too late. Caramel is being sold.

'Is there anything I can do or say to stop it?' I plead.

'Doubtful,' Kelly sighs. 'It's probably for the best, you know. Mr Seddon has trained horses before, and he knows what he's taking on – he'll get her settled down. He's rich – he's got a big house with paddocks and stables out Hartshill way. Don't worry, she'll have a good life.'

I'm not so sure. I didn't like the look of the posh, tweedy bloke – he seemed too sharp, too cold, his lips a thin, hard line. Besides, if he buys Caramel, I will never see her again.

✿✿✿✿✿✿✿✿✿✿✿✿✿✿✿✿✿✿✿✿✿✿✿✿

My eyes well with tears and Kelly, panicking, distracts me with a sharp burst of rising trot and a long canter across the meadows that edge the woods. Later, as we trek back through the trees towards the stable-yard gate, we see the shiny, silver four-wheel drive move out slowly, towing the horsebox.

I'm too late even to say goodbye.

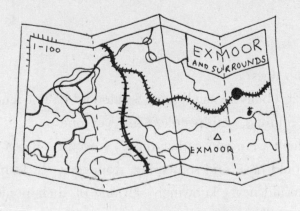

10

As I walk Bailey back to his stable, a figure steps out of the shadows.

'Well done, Coco,' Lawrie Marshall says coldly. 'Thanks to you, Caramel belongs to that thug Seddon now. Great stuff. Just great.'

'Thug?' I echo uneasily. 'Kelly says he's rich and knows loads about horses. She says Caramel will have a good life with him.'

'She obviously doesn't know him,' Lawrie says.

He turns away, stepping into Caramel's empty stable.

'What d'you mean, he's a thug?' I demand. 'You can't just make accusations like that! How do you even know?'

'I just know, all right?' he scowls, shovelling dirty straw. 'You don't like bullies, do you?'

'Who does?'

'Well, a bully is exactly what Seddon is,' Lawrie mutters. 'With animals, with people, with everyone.'

'Where were you earlier then?' I accuse. 'If it's true, you could have said something, stopped it all! Jean and Roy would never knowingly sell one of their ponies to someone like that!'

'Something came up,' he huffs. 'I'll make up the time, not that it's any of your business.'

'Have you told Jean and Roy what you know about Seddon?' I repeat.

'What's the point?' he shrugs. 'It's a done deal now. People like Seddon always get their way.'

He kicks the stable door closed, leaving me speechless.

I try to get the sharp face and cold eyes of the posh tweedy guy out of my mind, but I can't. Is he a rich guy who loves horses, like Kelly said, or a thug and a bully? I imagine him riding Caramel, tugging hard on the reins, digging his heels in, losing his temper if she is skittish.

Is he really bad news, or is Lawrie trying to wind me up? If so, it's working. I can't concentrate on anything. I have to trust Jean and Roy and Kelly. They would never let anyone dodgy buy Caramel, I am certain of that. Then again . . . what if Lawrie knows something that they don't?

'Maybe you could just ring Jean and Roy, explain that we're still interested in Caramel?' I ask Mum. 'In case things go wrong with her new home.'

Mum shakes her head. 'Coco, love, nothing will go wrong. I'd love for you to have a pony one day . . . in theory. But not the pony that threw you. And not right now. We are gearing up for the biggest order The Chocolate Box has ever had, and we need to focus on that for a while. Unless we do, there'll be no money for food and bills, let alone ponies!'

On Saturday morning I watch as endless deliveries of raw cocoa, sugar and flavourings arrive. One of the guest bedrooms is given over to towering piles of flat-packed boxes, ready to be assembled and filled. Paddy has enlisted extra help from Harry, the retired bloke from the village who helped out for three weeks back in the summer when Mum and Paddy went on their honeymoon. There is talk of a couple of part-timers being roped in, too, until this mammoth order has been filled.

71

❀❀❀❀❀❀❀❀❀❀❀❀❀❀❀❀❀❀❀❀❀❀❀❀❀❀❀

My sisters don't seem bothered by the chaos. Cherry is making her own magazine for an English project at school, spreading sketches and photos and chunks of printed-out writing across the kitchen table. Summer is practising barre exercises against the Aga and Skye is sitting in the armchair, sewing a 1920s-style dress from an old velvet curtain. Honey, needless to say, is still in bed.

Normally, I would be a part of it all, drafting out a petition about saving the Siberian white tiger or painting a banner to protest about testing make-up on animals, but today I haven't the heart for anything at all. All I can think about is Caramel, my mind racing with fears and worries and confusion.

Nobody notices that I'm upset. Nobody notices me at all – I am practically invisible.

On impulse, I grab the phone book and look up 'Seddon'. There is only one entry, a listing for J. Seddon at Blue Downs House, Hartshill. I take the old Ordnance Survey map from the living-room shelf and find the place, not far from Hartshill and maybe five or six miles from here. So near and yet so far.

❀❀❀❀❀❀❀❀❀❀❀❀❀❀❀❀❀❀❀❀❀❀❀

In the cold light of day, I am pretty sure that Caramel is fine. I am pretty sure that Lawrie Marshall is just a nasty, bitter kid who is trying to make me feel bad because I happened to find him bullying a Year Six boy. I try to forget Seddon's thin-lipped scowl, his ice-blue eyes.

I can't imagine Mr Seddon riding a small, stocky, half-wild Exmoor pony, though. Perhaps he has bought Caramel for one of his children? I picture Caramel being petted by a little boy with a face full of freckles, a cute grin. He would bring her carrots and peppermints and fresh hay, but would he know that apple slices are her favourite? Probably not.

And what if Caramel throws that cute, imaginary boy? What then?

'I'm going out,' I tell Mum. 'I might cycle up to town to see Sarah. I won't be late.'

I pull on my fluffy panda hat and slip out of the kitchen, wheel my bike out of the shed and start to cycle. I am not going to Sarah's house, though. It's a bright, crisp autumn day and I soon warm up as I ride down through the village and out again, taking the road to Hartshill.

I have no clear idea of what I will do when I get there, but I know I have to find Blue Downs House and see Caramel one last time, if only to say goodbye. Once I have seen her, I'll be able to let go, move on.

Maybe.

11

I take a right fork at the crossroads a mile before the village and head out towards the moorland. The cycling is harder now, and I have to get off and push the bike up some of the slopes. Cresting one windswept hill, I see a big whitewashed farmhouse in the valley below, a cobbled yard and some outbuildings and a paddock, flanked by woodland. Apart from a terrace of four pretty cottages further up the hill, the house is alone in the landscape, imposing and slightly forbidding.

I freewheel down the slope a little, skidding to a halt as I notice figures and a pony moving across the paddock in the distance. I step into the woodland, hiding my bike behind a mossy, tumbledown wall.

It's cold in the woods, and I move as quietly as I can,

twigs crackling and snapping underfoot, creeping forward until I can hear voices close by. Peering out from the fringe of trees, I see Mr Seddon standing in the centre of the paddock, a girl of seven or eight beside him. He is running Caramel on a long lunge line, turning slowly so that she trots in a circle round him.

I remember Kelly explaining that Mr Seddon has trained horses before, so I guess he is putting her through her paces, getting to know her. Caramel is trotting smoothly, but she looks tired, as if the training has been going on for a long time. The little girl's face looks grey and anxious, her lips quivering.

Suddenly a loud crack splits the air, and Caramel rears up, whinnying in distress. The sound rings out again, and I see that Seddon has a bullwhip, a huge, long-tailed whip that he is lashing out towards Caramel, who bucks to the side, trying to pull away. Seddon reels her in, then cracks his whip again, and this time the whiplash catches her flanks and I see the whites of her eyes as she struggles against the lunge line, terrified.

I want to run forward, into the paddock, grab the whip from Seddon and shove him away from Caramel, leave him sprawled on the ground in a puddle, red-faced and helpless. I want to wrench the lunge line from him and lead Caramel out of there, but fear and reason hold me back. I am twelve years old and all of five foot two inches tall. I don't honestly think I can fight some big, fierce bloke with a whip, no matter how much I want to.

I must not panic. I have to stay calm, think clearly, but it's easier said than done. I feel sick. Why would anyone deliberately frighten an already jumpy horse, then hit her when she flinches and bucks? My heart hammers so loudly I swear the world can hear it, but I force myself to be still, shielded by the trees.

'Stop it!' a voice appeals, and I see the little girl tugging at Seddon's sleeve. 'Please! Leave her alone!'

'She has to learn,' he snaps, shaking the child off. 'She's an animal, a wilful animal. She needs discipline!'

'You're hurting her!' the child argues. 'She's scared!'

'You wanted a pony, didn't you?' Seddon snaps.

'Yes, but –'

'But nothing,' he growls, cracking the whip again as Caramel trots forward, her eyes wild and frightened. 'This

77

❀❀❀❀❀❀❀❀❀❀❀❀❀❀❀❀❀❀❀❀❀❀❀❀

is how it works, Jasmine. Animals need to know who is master, and I am master here. Trust me, she will learn that. Sooner or later, she will learn.'

The child is crying now, trembling, her face streaked with tears. Seddon takes no notice, even when she sinks down to the ground, burying her face in her hands. He just goes on turning, stony-faced, running Caramel on her lunge line, on and on until I think she will fall to the ground too, exhausted.

At last, more than an hour later when the light begins to fade, Seddon stops. He pulls Caramel towards him, catching hold of her halter, and drags the little girl to her feet. I watch the three of them walk away, up towards the house, the stable yard.

Whatever I imagined when I tried to picture Caramel's new life, it wasn't this. There is no laughing, freckle-faced boy, no carrot treats or apple slices. And Seddon is exactly as Lawrie Marshall described him – a horrible, horrible bully. Well, it takes one to know one, I suppose.

I lean against a tree, trying to gather my wits. Should I call the RSPCA? Would they believe me? Would they think it was serious enough to take Caramel away from

❀❀❀❀❀❀❀❀❀❀❀❀❀❀❀❀❀❀❀❀❀❀❀

here, or would they just give Seddon a warning? What if he told them it was all lies?

Maybe ringing Jean and Roy at Woodlands would be better. They would hate to think that Caramel was being badly treated – maybe they could take her back again? I frown. Seddon has paid good money for Caramel, so I don't imagine he would be willing to let her go.

I can't risk leaving Caramel here – I have to get her out, no matter what.

A plan begins to unfurl in my mind. I sink down on to a fallen log, taking the little mobile I was given for my twelfth birthday and clicking on to Cherry's number. After three rings, my stepsister answers.

'It's me – Coco,' I say, huddling into my jacket. 'Are you alone? Can you talk? Because I need a favour. And it has to be a secret!'

'Coco? Yes, I'm in my room, but . . . what d'you mean? Where are you? What secret? And . . . why me?'

I roll my eyes. 'You're the only one who takes me seriously in this family,' I explain. 'Look . . . I need you to cover for me. I wouldn't ask, but it's *really* important. Life and death.'

❀❀❀❀❀❀❀❀❀❀❀❀❀❀❀❀❀❀❀❀❀❀❀❀

'*What?*' Cherry gasps.

'Chill out,' I say. 'I'm fine. But I need you to tell Mum and Paddy that I rang, and that I'm staying over with Sarah.'

'Aren't you with her?'

'Obviously not,' I say. 'Look, if you can just tell Mum –'

'What is going on? Where *are* you? And where are you staying tonight, if you're not coming home and you're not with Sarah?'

'I will be coming home,' I sigh. 'I promise. But it will be very late, and I don't want Mum to worry. I'll sleep in the gypsy caravan. I will explain everything when I see you. You have to trust me, Cherry, OK?'

'Oh, Coco!' she says. 'Are you in trouble?'

'No, no, I'm fine,' I insist. 'Honestly. I'll explain everything tomorrow. Will you cover for me, Cherry, please?'

There is a silence, and then I hear her sigh.

'Do you promise me you're not in any kind of trouble?' she asks.

'I'm fine,' I insist. 'It's no big deal, honestly, and I really will explain everything when I see you . . . please, Cherry?'

❀❀❀❀❀❀❀❀❀❀❀❀❀❀❀❀❀❀❀❀❀❀❀

I can just picture my stepsister's face, trying to balance concern with sisterly support and failing miserably.

'OK,' she says reluctantly. 'I'll tell Dad and Charlotte that you're staying with Sarah tonight. But . . . Coco? Whatever you're up to, be careful. OK?'

'I will,' I promise. 'Thanks, Cherry!'

I click to disconnect the call, then ring Sarah to make sure she will cover for me too if Mum should call her place to check. That's unlikely Sarah and I often sleep over at each other's houses, so it's no big deal – but I need to be sure. I tell her I am on a secret mission against animal cruelty, and that I will explain everything at school on Monday. Sarah offers to come and help, and I am tempted to let her, but then she remembers that her bike has a flat tyre.

'I could ask Dad for a lift?' she suggests. I tell her to forget it – asking for lifts after dark to the middle of nowhere would be way too suspicious.

'Sure?' she presses. 'I could bring a flask of soup. And blankets. And torches!'

I wish I had all of those things. I wish I had a friend to sit beside me in the woods as the night sky darkens

❀❀❀❀❀❀❀❀❀❀❀❀❀❀❀❀❀❀❀❀❀❀❀

and the cold seeps into my bones, but it looks like I am on my own with this.

'I'll be OK,' I say gruffly. 'No problem.'

After I ring off, Sarah and I text back and forth for a while, until she is called down for dinner and a DVD. I imagine my sisters, gathered round the table at Tanglewood, talking, laughing, eating, warm from the Aga. I imagine them stretched out on the squashy blue sofas, watching TV, squabbling about who should make the hot chocolates, whether it's time for bed.

An owl swoops by silently overhead, white wings beating as it navigates the trees, making me jump. I wish I was at home with my sisters, not huddled into my jacket, leaning against a tree, in the woods miles from home, waiting for midnight.

12

In the end, I don't make it quite that long. I doze a little and wake with a crick in my neck and an imprint of beech bark along my cheek, so cold I think I may be frozen to the spot. If I don't move soon the search parties will find me, a few days from now, a huddled figure in a panda hat, dead from the cold and lack of hot chocolate. I stand up and rub my hands together to get the circulation moving, stamp my feet on the litter of fallen leaves and broken twigs.

My mobile says it is ten forty-five, but I can still see lights in the windows of Blue Downs House. Surely they'll be getting ready for bed soon?

I make my way out of the woods and walk alongside the paddock, creeping closer to the house. Everything is quiet. I stand for a while at the stable-yard gate, listening, watching. Inside the house, someone draws the upstairs curtains, switches off a light. I see the silhouette of a woman pass one of the downstairs windows, carrying two glasses.

A dog, tied up in the yard, sniffs the air and looks towards me, straining at its rope. *Don't bark*, I tell the dog, silently. *Please, don't bark . . .*

I think I hear a movement somewhere near the stables, but although I listen hard for more sounds and stare into the darkness for any sign of movement, there is nothing. Probably just Caramel shifting around in her stall.

I open the gate carefully, leave it ajar and walk slowly, quietly, across the yard. The dog, a thin, bedraggled mongrel, watches my progress keenly. It yaps once, but quietens when I begin talking to it in a low whisper, gently. Dogs are quite like people. If you come across an angry one, you can sometimes calm it down by acting cool and confident yourself – although this dog doesn't seem angry, just thin and lonely and perhaps a little scared.

I cross the yard and peep into the first stable, but it's empty, as is the second. Approaching the third, I inhale the sweet hay-and-treacle smell of pony.

84

❁❁❁❁❁❁❁❁❁❁❁❁❁❁❁❁❁❁❁❁❁❁❁❁❁

'Caramel?' I whisper, pushing open the stable door.

A tall shadow looms at me in the dark and I am so shocked and scared I lose the plot completely, jumping back against the stable door.

'Whaaat the – urgghhh!' I yelp, and a hand clamps down across my mouth so that the last word dies a muffled death.

'Shut up!' a gruff voice tells me. 'You'll wake the whole place up!'

'Mnnnhh?' I grunt, wriggling free and turning on my captor. My eyes open wide.

'Lawrie Marshall?'

'You again!' he mutters. 'Unreal. Are you stalking me or something?'

Indignation just about chokes me.

'Stalk *you*?' I hiss. 'Get a life, Lawrie – are you crazy? I'm here for Caramel, obviously. What are *you* doing here?'

Lawrie sighs, and I look past him into the darkness to where Caramel is eating from a bucket of grain. I'm pretty sure Seddon didn't give her that . . . I guess Lawrie cares about the pony too.

85

✿✿✿✿✿✿✿✿✿✿✿✿✿✿✿✿✿✿✿✿✿✿✿✿✿✿

'You were right about Seddon,' I admit. 'I was watching him earlier, running Caramel in the paddock. He's horrible! Do you think we should ring the RSPCA?'

'That would only make things worse,' Lawrie says. 'You have no idea how powerful Seddon is. He owns a lot of land around here, knows all the right people. He's clever too, and he gets away with murder. He hasn't left a mark on Caramel, so it would be our word against his. Who do you think they'd believe? There's not much we can actually do except make sure she's fed properly . . . she was really hungry.'

Caramel lifts her head and mooches over to greet me, nuzzling her head against my cheek. I put my arms round her and hold her close, hoping she knows just how sorry I am. I think of her earlier, eyes wide with fear, and I know I cannot walk away and leave her here.

'Not much we can do?' I challenge Lawrie. 'I think there's plenty, actually. We can get Caramel out – ride her out of here, rescue her. Are you going to help?'

'Rescue?' he repeats. 'Steal, you mean! Are you serious?'

'Why not? Seddon may have paid for her, but he bought

Caramel under false pretences – Jean and Roy would never have let her go if they'd known what a creep he is. We can't leave her here, Lawrie!'

He frowns. 'Seddon really is bad news, y'know,' he tells me. 'He runs pheasant shoots for groups of toffs from the city, so he has a gun. Stealing something of his is not a good idea.'

'Do you have a better one?'

Lawrie laughs, and for a moment, in the shadowy stable, I catch a glimpse of the boy he could be if he wasn't always cross and scowling. His whole face lights up – it's kind of surprising.

'So . . . we're doing this?' he checks.

'I'm doing it,' I shrug. 'You can please yourself.'

I saddle Caramel quickly, then take her head collar and lead her forward, out into the yard. The dog stares at us, forlorn, but Lawrie talks to it in a low whisper and it makes no attempt to bark as we latch the stable-yard gate behind us and make for the woods.

'What now?' Lawrie asks as we step into the safety of the trees. 'Do you have a plan?'

'I'm going to hide Caramel in the stables at home,' I

reply. 'Our pet sheep Humbug lives there at the moment, but I am pretty sure she won't mind sharing.'

'What will you tell your parents?'

'I'm not sure yet,' I admit. 'This is a spur of the moment thing, I haven't had a chance to plan out the details . . .'

'Not going to work,' he says. 'Trust me, Seddon will go crazy once he discovers Caramel is gone. He'll get the police involved, the newspapers, you name it. Your parents would know exactly what had happened, and I bet they'd hand Caramel straight back. Even if they didn't want to, the police would probably make them. No, if we're going to help Caramel, we need to hide her – somewhere nobody will find her.'

'Where, though?' I ask. 'A pony is pretty hard to hide!'

Lawrie frowns, thoughtful.

'I know a place. But if we're really doing this . . . well, there's something else you should see.'

'What do you mean?'

Lawrie ties Caramel's reins to a branch and grabs my hand in the darkness. Shock and annoyance flood through me, but before I can argue or swat him away he pulls me out of the trees and into the farmyard, dropping my

❀❀❀❀❀❀❀❀❀❀❀❀❀❀❀❀❀❀❀❀❀❀❀❀❀

hand again and pushing open the door of the fourth stable. In the darkness, I breathe in the warm, slightly treacly smell of horse mixed with the sour ammoniac reek of wet straw.

'Another horse?' I whisper.

Lawrie flicks on a torch, lighting up a bedraggled dapple-grey pony cowering in the far corner of the stall. Her belly is round as a barrel, and her eyes flare with fear as she begins skittering, jostling, trying to back away.

'She's terrified!' I say.

'And she's in foal,' Lawrie points out. 'Seddon bought her cheap, and he's totally neglected her.'

I look at the startled pony and bite my lip. Rescuing one pony or rescuing two . . . what's the difference?

'Lawrie,' I say, 'we'll have to take her too. We can't leave her here!'

'Thought you'd say that,' he huffs, and I can't tell whether he is pleased or irritated by my decision. 'Suppose we might as well be hung for a sheep as a lamb . . .'

He moves forward slowly, talking softly to the pony, offering her grain, clipping a leading rein on to her head collar. Jumpy and afraid, she still allows Lawrie to lead

✿✿✿✿✿✿✿✿✿✿✿✿✿✿✿✿✿✿✿✿✿✿✿✿

her out of the stable and into the woods. I wonder just how this boy can be so good with horses and yet so awkward with people?

Half an hour later Lawrie is riding Caramel uphill through moonlit fields while I trudge along behind with the dapple-grey mare. Lawrie Marshall has not only hijacked my plan but taken charge of it – he really is the most annoying boy I know.

'You're good,' I tell him grudgingly, as I guide the frightened grey forward. 'Have you worked with horses before?'

'Loads,' he shrugs. 'Up until I came to Somerset, anyhow.'

'Where are we going?'

'You'll see . . .'

We go on, cross-country in the moonlight for a mile or so, until we are high up on the moors, scrunching through heather and bracken, listening to the drumming cry of grouse and the soft huffing of the ponies' breath as they climb. Just when I am losing the will to live, the dark shape of a house appears in the distance, and Lawrie swings down from the saddle.

'They should be OK here,' he says. 'This place was a smallholding once, but it's been derelict for years – there's no proper road to it, you see. The ponies can go in the walled garden – it's all closed in and overgrown. Nobody would think of looking there – it's miles from the roads and there aren't any paths or tracks nearby, so hikers and tourists don't really bother with it. I'll bring them some grain and stuff tomorrow.'

'We will,' I correct him. 'This rescue was my idea, remember?'

'How could I forget?' Lawrie sighs. 'OK. Can you be here for half two-ish, d'you think?'

'I suppose,' I say, shivering a little in the moonlight. 'This place is spooky.'

'It's safe,' Lawrie shrugs. 'That's what matters, isn't it?'

For once in his life, I guess Lawrie is right.

13

I wake late, shivering under the quilt in the gypsy caravan with Fred the dog burrowed underneath the duvet. When the door opens and Cherry comes in with French toast and hot chocolate I think I've died and gone to heaven.

'You're awake,' she grins. 'I peeped in earlier, and you were still out for the count.'

I have no idea what time I finally made it home last night. By the time I'd trekked back over the moors to retrieve my bike from Blue Downs House and pedalled home in the moonlight, I was exhausted. I crept into the gypsy caravan, crawled under the covers and slept. I dreamt of Caramel and the dapple-grey mare galloping free across the moors, and then the dream turned into a nightmare and I was running through the darkness, lost, alone, being chased by horrible Mr Seddon and his shotgun.

Not good. I push the thought away.

'You are officially the best stepsister I have ever had,' I say to Cherry, reaching for the hot chocolate. 'Thank you!'

'I'm the *only* stepsister you've ever had,' she laughs. 'And I'm glad you slept well because I didn't – I was worried sick! Tell me what you were doing, Coco, please?'

'Promise you won't say anything to anyone?' I check. 'Seriously – you have to keep it secret. Sisters don't tell, right?'

Cherry frowns. 'I guess,' she shrugs. 'But . . . it's nothing awful, is it? Illegal?'

I tell Cherry the story of Caramel's rescue and her eyes open wide.

'It is illegal,' she whispers, horrified. 'But I can see exactly why you did it. Poor Caramel!'

I sip my hot chocolate. 'Actually, it wasn't just Caramel. There was another pony too – a pregnant mare. We couldn't leave her behind!'

93

❀❀❀❀❀❀❀❀❀❀❀❀❀❀❀❀❀❀❀❀❀❀❀

Cherry frowns. 'Two ponies? Be careful, Coco. That Seddon bloke sounds like a total creep. I think you should tell Dad and Charlotte!'

'But Seddon will report the theft and get the police involved,' I argue. 'And Mum and Paddy would make me give the ponies back. Adults always stick together!'

'Dad and Charlotte would understand, if you explained it properly,' Cherry says. 'They'd know what to do.'

I bite my lip. 'I can't,' I say. 'I promised Lawrie.'

Cherry frowns. 'So who is this Lawrie person?' she asks. 'Do I know him?'

'I don't think so,' I frown. 'He joined the middle school last year – moved from up north, I think, judging by his accent. He's a bit of a mystery boy.'

'They're the ones to watch out for,' Cherry says darkly. 'Tread carefully, Coco. This stunt with the horses is serious stuff – I bet you anything it will make the papers, cause a big fuss with the police. You could get into a whole heap of trouble. I mean, it's OK to like a boy, have a crush even, but don't let him lead you astray.'

I just about choke on my hot chocolate.

'Er, *no way* do I fancy Lawrie Marshall,' I snort. 'He is

❀❀❀❀❀❀❀❀❀❀❀❀❀❀❀❀❀❀❀❀❀❀❀

the most obnoxious, irritating boy in the world. Horrible and arrogant and rude.'

Cherry looks unconvinced.

'I mean it,' I argue. 'Not. Interested. End of story. Besides, Lawrie is *not* leading me astray – the rescue was all my idea. I agree with him about keeping it quiet, though. We can't let Seddon get his hands on Caramel again. As for the other pony, she was terrified – I can't let them go back there. We have to keep them hidden, for now at least – I'll make sure they're fed and groomed. I'll think of a better plan soon, but right now this has to stay secret. You won't give me away, will you?'

My stepsister bites her lip. 'I suppose not,' she promises. 'But I don't like this, Coco. Technically, it's stealing, and if anyone finds out you were involved . . .'

'They won't.'

Cherry sighs. 'You've rescued the ponies, and that's great, but . . . I think you should tell the authorities now. Caramel isn't your responsibility, and the other one definitely isn't – you shouldn't get in too deep!'

But I am already in too deep, and there is no turning back.

95

❀❀❀❀❀❀❀❀❀❀❀❀❀❀❀❀❀❀❀❀❀❀❀❀❀

By the time I'm up and dressed, Tanglewood is in chaos. As usual, my sisters are so wrapped up in their own lives they barely notice me at all, and Mum and Paddy are interviewing people from the village to help them fill the big chocolate order. Even if I did want to confide in them, I doubt if they'd have time to listen. They either fuss over me as if I am three years old or else barely notice I'm alive. Right now, though, all this is working to my advantage – nobody except Cherry has the slightest idea I've been up to anything.

The interviews are all done by midday, and we gather round the kitchen table for a healthy brunch. Even Honey has made an effort and put in an appearance, smiling and helpful, doing her best impression of the perfect daughter.

We feast on fresh fruit and yoghurt, then Mum's special eggs Florentine, a poached egg, spinach and mushroom combo that everybody loves. Our meals are extra healthy these days because of Summer's eating disorder – although she doesn't eat very much of anything, just picks at her fruit and manages a few forkfuls of poached egg. We are

96

not allowed to mention this in case it makes her feel bad and makes her eat even less, but trust me, it is not easy watching your beautiful sister surviving on strawberries and fresh air. Apparently the twice-a-week day clinic is helping her get back into healthier eating patterns, but I can't see an awful lot of progress myself. Mum says that battling an eating disorder takes time.

Sometimes I wonder what would have happened if nobody had noticed what Summer was doing, if she'd packed her bags and headed off to dance school this September as she was supposed to. Even the thought of it scares me half to death.

'We need you girls to be patient, these next few weeks,' Paddy is saying, helping himself to a slice of toast. 'Charlotte and I will be working flat out to get this chocolate order sorted, so things could be hectic. We'll need you all to bear with us.'

'Don't worry,' Skye says. 'We'll all help.'

'Just tell us what needs doing,' Summer agrees, and I have to bite my tongue to stop myself from pointing out the irony of my anorexic sister offering to help out with the chocolate business. It's kind of sick.

✿ ✿

Mum pours more orange juice. 'I think we have the production side of things pretty much covered,' she says. 'We've signed up enough part-time workers to do three shifts a day, morning, afternoon and evening. If things go according to plan we should be able to meet the order in time and get those chocolates on the shelves by the end of the month. Paddy and I will be busier than usual, but there are no B&B bookings over the next couple of weeks, and we won't take any more until all this is over, so . . .'

'So it's just us,' Cherry states. 'Don't worry, we'll manage fine. We were OK while you two were on honeymoon, weren't we?'

That's not strictly true – Grandma Kate came over to keep an eye on us back then. Besides, Summer's freaky food phobia started while Mum and Paddy were away in August, and Honey used their absence as an excuse to go off the rails again. She almost burnt the stable block down one night and Summer had to go to hospital with smoke inhalation, although they did find out about her eating disorder while she was there so it wasn't all bad.

Still, I am not sure the honeymoon is a good example of us managing on our own.

Mum seems to agree. 'Well,' she frowns, 'it won't be quite like that. Paddy and I will be busy, but we're right here if you need us. I'll be running Summer to and from Exeter to the clinic as usual. You girls come first!'

Her eyes flicker over Summer, who is cutting a grilled tomato into careful quarters, spearing a few swirls of spinach but not actually eating anything.

'We'll be fine, Mum,' Summer says quietly.

'Sure you will,' she says brightly. 'I've stocked up the freezer, but you might have to keep a check that you've got clean clothes for school and shout out if you need anything. We'll all muddle through. Right?'

'Right,' Honey says. 'Don't stress, Mum. It's only for a couple of weeks – no hassle! The place will run like clockwork, I'll see to that.'

Mum smiles. 'I know you will, Honey,' she says. 'We're so pleased with your report – just look what you can achieve when you try! I'm so proud of you!'

'Whatever,' my big sister says, her cheeks flushing pink, either with modesty or guilt. 'I just want you to know you can rely on us to cope with stuff here. OK, you lot?'

❀❀❀❀❀❀❀❀❀❀❀❀❀❀❀❀❀❀❀❀❀

'OK,' I chime in with my sisters. 'No worries.'

Honey, Cherry and Skye look unconcerned, but I notice that Summer's eyes are shadowed with uncertainty. Me, I can't help thinking that dealing with two rescued ponies will be a whole lot easier while Mum and Paddy are run off their feet. The busier they are, the less likely they are to notice my comings and goings.

I take a deep breath.

'I'm going down to the village in a bit,' I say casually. 'To see Jayde and Amy. Is that OK?'

Cherry shoots me a questioning look, but I avoid her eyes and Mum just nods and tells me to make sure I'm not too late back, to call if I need a lift. I promise I will, but of course I won't need a lift because I'm not going to see my friends, I'm going up to the derelict cottage. I have already hidden my bike down behind the gypsy caravan, my rucksack dangling from the handlebars, stuffed with hay and apples.

I am not sure when I got to be so good at lying. It's like I am turning into a mini version of my big sister, only with save-the-whale tendencies and flatter shoes. Honey is turning over a new leaf, while I am flinging

✿✿✿✿✿✿✿✿✿✿✿✿✿✿✿✿✿✿✿✿✿✿✿✿

myself headlong into a whole lot of trouble. I have never been afraid to stand up for animals, but even I know stealing ponies is serious. It makes baking cakes to raise money for the pandas look like kid's stuff.

After brunch, I curl up in the oak tree to play my violin, but I can't concentrate; my mind is full of stolen ponies, angry landowners, surly boys. I check my watch, killing time until I can set off for the derelict cottage. I am kicking at the red-gold foliage, anxious, edgy, when Honey walks across the grass wearing a cute print minidress, mustard-coloured tights and high-heeled, lace-up boots. She leans up against the tree trunk, and takes a compact mirror out of her bag to paint on scarlet lipstick and shimmery gold eyeshadow.

Watching all this through the branches, I can't help thinking she is taking an awful lot of trouble to look cool and pretty for a girl who is grounded until Christmas.

Maybe I was wrong about the new-leaf thing?

'Going somewhere nice?' I ask, and Honey yelps, dropping her eyeshadow into the grass.

'Coco, you are such a freak,' she huffs, scooping it up and stuffing it into her handbag. 'What is it with you and

❁ ❁

trees? Are you actually part monkey?'

'Stop changing the subject,' I say. 'I thought you were grounded?'

'I'm just going down to Anthony's,' she tells me. 'Mum knows, and she says it's fine. He's helping me with my calculus homework, OK? I want to get good grades.'

I frown. Anthony is Kitnor's only teen maths and computer genius, one of those slightly eccentric boys who still lets his mum cut his hair in a little-boy bowl haircut and never seems to notice that his shirt tails are hanging. I think he has a bit of a crush on Honey, but it's definitely a one-way thing.

Besides, Honey doesn't look like she's dressed to walk down to the village to study calculus.

'Is Anthony your boyfriend now then?' I ask, swinging my legs just above her head.

'That's sick!' she squeals, outraged. 'Of course he isn't. I'm just studying, OK? Nothing else.'

She picks her way across the grass and I hear the gate creak as she steps out on to the lane, the clack-clack of her high-heeled boots on tarmac. As I listen, a car draws up blaring music and voices call out, laughing, telling

❀❀❀❀❀❀❀❀❀❀❀❀❀❀❀❀❀❀❀❀❀❀❀

Honey to jump in. 'Shhh!' I hear her hiss. 'My little sister is lurking about – keep the noise down! I'm grounded, remember!'

A door slams and the car accelerates away, and I am left with a sinking feeling. New leaf? Honey? That'll be the day.

14

It's eerily quiet as I cycle along the lanes towards the moors. It's not such a long ride as yesterday – according to Lawrie, the derelict farm is almost halfway between Hartshill and Kitnor as the crow flies, so I take the route Lawrie has suggested, staying well away from Blue Downs House. Once I reach the uplands I hide my bike in a coppice of hazel trees he told me to look for and find a tiny stream that is supposed to lead right up to the derelict cottage.

I leave the lane behind and begin to trek upwards, following the silver ribbon of stream as it cuts through the heather and bracken. Each step feels like freedom, like leaving the chaos of the big chocolate order and Summer's illness and Honey's latest rule-breaking all behind me. There is nobody else around, and all I can hear is the distant buzz of a car down below, the screech of geese flying overhead, the rhythm of my footsteps as I walk.

At one point I glimpse a herd of wild Exmoor ponies in the distance, their dark manes ruffled by the breeze as they watch me pass. If all else fails, maybe I could set Caramel loose on the moors and hope that she finds them? It would break my heart, but at least she'd be safe. That wouldn't work for the grey, of course – she's not an Exmoor, and her colour would mark her out from the herd instantly.

I am just beginning to worry that I'm following the wrong stream when the tumbledown smallholding appears in the distance. In the daylight I can see a rectangle of drystone wall enclosing an overgrown field and tall, ivy-covered walls shielding the garden. When I get closer, I notice a tatty red sign that reads *Danger: Unsafe Building* tied to the cast-iron gate.

As I duck through the gate a tangle of starry white jasmine flowers brushes against my face, the remnants of a long-forgotten garden now running wild. The air smells

❁❁❁❁❁❁❁❁❁❁❁❁❁❁❁❁❁❁❁❁❁❁❁

heady, musky, sweet, and everything seems peaceful in the fading sun – it's the kind of place where time stands still.

Walking along the overgrown path, I see another sign, fixed above the broken doorway, faded, the paint peeling. *Jasmine Cottage.* I think again of the little girl with Seddon yesterday, her pale face stained with tears. He called her Jasmine.

Who lived here, long ago? Was there a family, kids playing in the stream, parents tending the vegetable garden, a couple of cows and sheep in the field, ducks and chickens perhaps? What became of them? Perhaps the children grew up and headed for the city, leaving their parents to grow old alone, their home falling into disrepair around them.

What would they think of our kidnap, the hidden ponies?

'Hello?' I call, and Caramel comes trotting towards me through the tangle of undergrowth, pushing her nose against my shoulder and making soft, whickering sounds as I stroke her neck.

'Oh, Caramel,' I whisper into her mane. 'I'm so, so sorry . . .'

✿✿✿✿✿✿✿✿✿✿✿✿✿✿✿✿✿✿✿✿✿✿✿

After a while I step back, taking an apple from my rucksack and cutting it into slices to feed to her.

The dapple-grey mare appears behind Caramel, shy and jittery. She seems too nervous to approach, but I stay still and quiet, my arm outstretched, the juicy apple slices on my open palm, tempting her. I have learnt that when an animal is frightened, the best way forward is to let it come to you; after a while she edges close enough to take the apple, her nose like warm velvet against my skin, her breath soft and warm.

'Nice job,' a voice says behind me, and I turn to see Lawrie Marshall sitting on the window sill of the derelict cottage. 'That one's really wary of people . . . with good cause, obviously. We'll probably never know her real story.'

'At least now we know it has a happy ending,' I comment.

'Well, maybe,' Lawrie says. 'Having a mare in foal really complicates things. She's not in great condition and I've no idea when she's due to foal. What if we're lumped with delivering it?'

'We'd manage,' I say bravely, although I am starting to feel a little out of my depth.

✿✿✿✿✿✿✿✿✿✿✿✿✿✿✿✿✿✿✿✿✿✿✿✿

'Maybe,' Lawrie says. 'Right now, anything we can do to rebuild her trust has to help. You've got patience – maybe even a way with animals. I suppose everyone has at least *some* good points.'

'Even me?' I huff. 'Careful. You almost said something nice then. Are you feeling ill or something?'

'Funny,' Lawrie says. 'Look, I didn't ask to be in this mess with you, you know. I can manage fine on my own if there's something else you'd rather be doing.'

'That's rich!' I splutter. 'Whose idea was this rescue? Mine, Lawrie Marshall, OK? If it wasn't for me, they'd still be stuck with that creep Seddon, half-starved and treated like dirt, so don't you tell me to push off and go and do something else –'

'Calm down,' he says. 'I didn't say that. Look . . . can we try to get along? For the sake of the horses? I don't much like you and I know you don't like me –'

'That's the understatement of the year,' I snap.

'Fine,' Lawrie shrugs. 'Forget about getting along. Let's just work out what needs to be done. I've brought up a net of hay and some grain, plus buckets for water and feed . . .'

❀ ❀ ❀ ❀ ❀ ❀ ❀ ❀ ❀ ❀ ❀ ❀ ❀ ❀ ❀ ❀ ❀ ❀ ❀

I look around, taking in the feed buckets and the hay. My own effort – a rucksack filled with hay and apples – looks childish by comparison.

'Seddon must have noticed by now,' I say. 'He's bound to go to the police. Is it really safe to leave the ponies here?'

Lawrie shrugs. 'I think so. I've been up here tons of times over the summer and never seen another soul. Walkers usually stick to the pathways and the house is pretty much a wreck – dangerous too, most of it. The garden's secure and the wall is too high for anyone to notice the ponies from a distance, so I reckon they should be safe enough for now.'

'Won't Seddon search?' I frown. 'The police too?'

'They might,' Lawrie says. 'I just don't think they'd look here. They'll assume whoever stole the horses is planning to sell them on, profit from them somehow . . . not hide them out on the moors. Moving them both now would be a big risk, but if we sit tight and keep them here, they should be safe. Trust me.'

'Do I have a choice?'

Lawrie rolls his eyes. 'If you have a better plan, go

ahead and tell me,' he says. 'As long as it doesn't involve petitions or cupcakes iced with panda faces. And be careful what you tell your friends about this – one careless word could endanger these horses.'

'As if!' I protest. 'I'd never do anything to put them in danger.'

'If you do say anything about it, leave me out,' he adds. 'I don't want to be part of the gossip. This isn't a game, Coco . . . it's serious, or haven't you noticed?'

'Of course I've noticed,' I scowl. 'Don't worry, I won't exactly be spreading the word that you're involved. I did tell my stepsister Cherry, but she won't tell anyone – she promised.'

Lawrie curls his lip, as if he doesn't believe in promises, or in me for that matter.

'So, do we make a rota for coming up to feed and check on them?' I ask. 'Only it's getting dark quite early now that the clock's gone back, and school doesn't finish till half three, so . . .'

'Scared of the dark, are you?' Lawrie shakes his head. 'Don't worry, I'll bring up lanterns and candles, and you should carry a torch, obviously. How long did it take you

❀❀❀❀❀❀❀❀❀❀❀❀❀❀❀❀❀❀❀❀❀

to cycle to the hazel copse? We can meet down there most days at maybe half four, if you're too chicken to come on your own. I'll come up on my own on Tuesdays and Fridays, after work. Those can be your days off, and maybe you can do Saturdays for me in return? I have to take my little sister to dance class in Minehead on Saturday mornings.'

'No problem,' I say. 'I can do Sundays too, obviously, to keep it fair.'

'We can take turns,' he shrugs. 'Whatever.'

I bite my lip, glad to know I don't have to hike across the moors in the dark, alone – even if my companion happens to be the scratchiest, spikiest boy in Somerset.

'I didn't know you had a little sister,' I say, wondering how she puts up with him.

'There's a lot you don't know about me,' he replies. 'She's eight. I buy your cakes for her sometimes. She likes them, even the ridiculous panda-face ones.'

'You say the sweetest things,' I huff. 'There was me thinking you cared about the plight of the giant panda. Another illusion shattered.'

Lawrie gets to his feet, gazing into the dusk at the two

❀ ❀

ponies grazing the knee-high grass. 'It's these two I'm bothered about right now,' he tells me. 'We may have got them away from Seddon, but we have to keep them safe and work out what to do with them. I don't suppose your plan goes that far?'

'Not yet,' I admit. 'I'm working on it.'

'Work fast then,' he says. 'These two ponies are trouble. One of them is unpredictable, unrideable; the other run-down, neglected, terrified of humans and in foal. They don't stand much chance of finding a happy-ever-after home if you ask me. That's the trouble with bullies like Seddon – the damage they do goes on and on.'

I raise an eyebrow. 'Not keen on bullies, all of a sudden?' I ask.

'Not keen on them, ever,' he says. 'I know you think I am one, but you couldn't be more wrong. That day you found me scrapping with Darren Holmes from Year Six . . . well, I'd just stopped him nicking a tinful of crispy cakes from some Year Five girl. He's the bully, and for the record, he's the one who hoisted your panda hat up the school flagpole too –'

❀❀❀❀❀❀❀❀❀❀❀❀❀❀❀❀❀❀❀❀❀❀❀

'Hang on!' I interrupt. 'That kid you had by the collar –
he was the bully?'

'That's right,' Lawrie says. 'OK, I probably shouldn't
have grabbed him like that. I know I shouldn't. Makes
me no better than Seddon, I guess. But . . . sometimes
you just see red. I saw that Year Five girl and I thought,
y'know, she could have been my sister – I couldn't let
him get away with it!'

Shame floods me as I remember wading in to drag
Lawrie away from the weaselly Year Six boy. How did I
get it so wrong? Instead of stopping a bully, I helped one
escape.

'But . . . why didn't you tell me?' I stammer. 'You let
me say all kinds of stuff – I feel awful now! I remember
the little girl too. She was buying the cakes for her mum's
birthday.'

'Most of them ended up in a puddle,' he shrugs. 'I
didn't tell you because . . . well, you wouldn't have listened,
would you? People like you never do. For the record, I
hate bullies just as much as you do. More, actually. I can
guarantee that. OK?'

I blink. What does that even mean? I look at Lawrie,

❀❀❀❀❀❀❀❀❀❀❀❀❀❀❀❀❀❀❀❀

taking in the proud set of his shoulders, the defiant tilt of his chin, the way his fringe flops down over his face, shadowing his eyes and giving him a distant, stay-away vibe. The look I mistook for surly aggression – could it be more about self-defence? He is still quite new at Exmoor Park Middle School, and nobody seems to know much about him. Perhaps he has been bullied himself?

Guilt lodges itself in my throat, awkward, embarrassing.

'Look, I'm sorry if I got it all wrong, I really didn't mean . . .'

Lawrie brushes off my apology. 'It's over now. Forget it. The ponies are fed and watered and safe. It's getting dark; we should head down to the road.'

How do you say sorry to someone who thinks you're annoying, who won't let anyone get close?

I duck out through the rusty iron gate, stopping to pick a tangle of jasmine flowers as I go. Their rich scent wraps itself around me as I follow Lawrie Marshall slowly across the dark moor, keeping the silver-glinting stream to our right. When we reach the road, I shove the bunch of starry white flowers at him, grabbing my bike.

'For your sister,' I blurt. 'She might like them.'

❀ ❀

I think of another little girl, scared and crying, watching her dad training Caramel to the point of exhaustion, and I pedal hard all the way home, dynamo lights flickering in the moonlight.

15

On Monday lunchtime, I call an emergency meeting of the Save the Animals Club. I drag Sarah, Amy and Jayde down to the edge of the playing fields and into the woods that skirt the school boundary.

'Why here?' Amy is complaining, her Ugg boots sinking into wet leaves. 'Why not the school canteen, or a corner of Mr Wolfe's classroom? This is crazy!'

'And cold,' Sarah grumbles as we settle ourselves on to fallen logs and huddle into our coats. 'Plus, we are breaking school rules – we're not allowed in the woods outside of PE cross-country lessons, Coco, you know that!'

'Which means it should be safe,' I point out. 'This is important!'

'It had better be,' Jayde huffs, snuggling into her scarf.

❁❁❁❁❁❁❁❁❁❁❁❁❁❁❁❁❁❁❁❁❁❁❁

'If you've brought us out here to start telling us about the plight of the South American great crested newt or the Siberian mongoose, I will not be happy!'

I wish my friends were a bit more supportive sometimes. They used to care about endangered wildlife and animal cruelty as much as I did, or almost; but over the last year they have totally lost the plot. Lately, they spend more time giggling about boys or flicking through the pages of the latest teen mags, discussing music videos or fashion or glittery nail varnish. I despair of them sometimes.

I watch, exasperated, as Jayde takes out a dog-eared romance paperback and Amy flicks open a compact mirror to apply a slick of lipgloss. At least Sarah is listening, for now.

'I'm not actually sure there are great crested newts in South America, but anyway, it's nothing like that,' I say. 'This is much closer to home. It's big news – I happen to know that local animal rights activists rescued two ill-treated ponies from Blue Downs House this weekend.'

Jayde drops her paperback into the fallen leaves.

'Wow,' she breathes. 'Really?'

❀❀❀❀❀❀❀❀❀❀❀❀❀❀❀❀❀❀❀❀❀❀❀❀❀

'Blue Downs?' Amy echoes, snapping shut her compact mirror. 'That's near Hartshill, I think.'

Sarah doesn't say anything, but her eyes narrow – I know that she is remembering Saturday's phone call and texts, when I told her I was on a secret mission.

'These local animal rights activists,' she says. 'Let's see. They would be . . . *you*, Coco, right?'

'Well . . . sort of!'

My three friends sit up straight, eyes wide. They are looking at me with a kind of admiration, which feels weird but nice.

'No way,' Jayde gasps. 'You rescued two ponies? By yourself?'

I bite my lip. It feels wrong taking all the credit, but Lawrie was very definite about not wanting to be mentioned.

'I had to,' I say. 'They were being ill-treated – anyone would have done the same. They are in a safe place for now, obviously, but this has to stay secret. I can trust you, right?'

'Of course,' Amy says. 'We won't breathe a word! Wow, Coco, I just can't believe you did that, all by yourself!'

❀❀❀❀❀❀❀❀❀❀❀❀❀❀❀❀❀❀❀❀❀❀

'Safest way,' I shrug, feeling guilty at the lie but pleased to have their attention again. Of course, if they knew Lawrie was involved in the rescue, I'd have their attention all right – but not in a good way. I give my friends an edited version of the kidnap, and they promise to keep my secret, offering to chip in with apples, carrots and alibis in case I need to come up with excuses for Mum and Paddy.

'If the police come asking, we'll say you were with us,' Sarah offers. 'A sleepover, or something. Maybe we could say we were up till midnight, and that we looked out of the window and saw a big horsebox driving past. That would put them off the scent. They'd assume the ponies were long gone then!'

'Maybe,' I say, but I know that an alibi like that would never hold water, not for long. 'Hopefully, the police won't actually question us.'

Distant shouts ring through the woods, and the sound of breaking twigs jolts us to our feet. 'Running club,' Jayde says, picking up her abandoned paperback. 'They practise on Monday lunchtimes. We'd better go.'

As we crunch back towards the school playing fields,

❀ ❀

we pass a couple of kids in running kit, red-faced and sweating, staggering in the opposite direction. 'Cross-country running ought to carry a government health warning,' Sarah muses. 'Look how red-faced and sweaty they get. And all that jiggling about can't be good for your insides!'

A lone figure crashes through the undergrowth and lopes towards us, long limbs pounding the muddy path. Lawrie Marshall doesn't look red-faced or sweaty, just predictably grim, dark wavy hair flopping across his face, blue eyes guarded. He spots me and shoots me a disgusted look, the kind that could shrivel an oak tree, which I think is a bit harsh after our adventures this weekend. He could at least be polite – I tilt my chin and refuse to be frozen out.

'Hello, Lawrie,' I say.

'All right,' he mutters, and thunders past, splattering me with mud from a nearby puddle. Typical.

'He spoke to you!' Amy whispers the minute Lawrie has gone. 'And you spoke to him. What's going on? I thought you couldn't stand him!'

'I can't,' I say. 'He drives me nuts. But I have decided

✿✿✿✿✿✿✿✿✿✿✿✿✿✿✿✿✿✿✿✿✿✿✿✿✿✿

not to let him get to me. If he scowls at me, I will smile. If he sneers, I will say hello. Why should I let him wind me up?'

'Right,' Jayde says. 'A new tactic – save the world with smiles. I like it!'

'Not sure it will work with loner-boy, though,' Sarah muses. 'Although he is quite good-looking, in a smouldering kind of way. Dark and brooding. Sort of wild!'

'What?' I frown. 'Lawrie Marshall? Are you mad?'

'The hero in this book is exactly the same,' Sarah tells me, waving her paperback in front of my nose. 'Moody and mysterious, but with hidden depths. Maybe Lawrie will ask you out. If he does, would you say yes?'

I will be spending most afternoons for the foreseeable future trudging across the moors with him, but Sarah doesn't need to know that.

'Of course not!' I scoff. 'Really, he's not interested – and nor am I. No way. I promise you, if Lawrie Marshall has hidden depths they are so well hidden that a whole team of archaeologists couldn't unearth them. Or whatever. Although personally, I am not sure he has any hidden depths at all . . .'

❀❀❀❀❀❀❀❀❀❀❀❀❀❀❀❀❀❀❀❀❀❀❀❀

I trail off into silence, aware that Sarah, Amy and Jayde are watching me keenly.

'You like him,' Amy says teasingly. 'I can tell!'

Instantly, the pony rescue is old news, replaced by a frenzied fascination for whether I am crushing on Lawrie Marshall. Why is everyone obsessed with boys all of a sudden? It's like the minute we all turned twelve, that's all anyone can think of. I am not totally immune to boys – I am only human, after all – but I am not about to let hormones rule my life. I have too many things to do to let boys get in the way. I have to save the whale and the tiger and the giant panda, then qualify as a vet, become a famous violinist and maybe start up my own sanctuary for ill-treated ponies as well. That doesn't leave a lot of time for romance.

Which is just as well, if Lawrie Marshall is the best candidate my friends can come up with.

'He's a mystery boy,' Sarah says thoughtfully, as we trudge back up to school across the playing fields. 'I mean, what do we actually know about him? Not much. He came here a year ago . . . didn't somebody say he was from the Lake District?'

'He used to look kind of scruffy,' Jayde adds. 'But these

❀❀❀❀❀❀❀❀❀❀❀❀❀❀❀❀❀❀❀❀❀❀❀❀

days he wears quite nice stuff. I think he's probably quite well off.'

'Don't know about that,' I say. 'He told me he's working at the stables because he needs the money.'

Amy grins. 'So you do talk to him! I knew it! And you have loads in common, like your shared love of horses . . .'

'We don't talk,' I correct her. 'He just snaps at me from time to time. That's not a conversation!'

But yesterday evening we managed at least two minutes of chat without descending back into sniping. Does that count?

'I see him getting out of a very posh four-wheel drive some mornings,' Sarah comments. 'So he can't exactly be poor.'

Lawrie Marshall is a mystery boy all right. Is he angry at the world or just trying to be invisible? Is he rich or poor, cruel or kind, secretive or just plain rude? He doesn't make it easy for anyone to get to know him and he's definitely not the friendliest boy I've ever met, but does that make him a bad person?

I cannot work it out.

'He fancies you, definitely,' Amy smirks. 'I can tell!'

✿✿✿✿✿✿✿✿✿✿✿✿✿✿✿✿✿✿✿✿✿✿✿✿

Sometimes I wonder if I am the only sane one on this whole planet, I swear.

Lawrie Marshall is waiting in the copse of hazel trees beneath the moor at half four, doing some maths homework. When he sees me he closes his exercise book and stuffs it into a rucksack, watching while I hide my bike in a clump of bushes. He falls into step beside me, following the stream across the moor.

'So,' he says, as if the whole day at school hasn't even happened, 'I hear Seddon's been to the police. They're making enquiries, planning a search.'

'They mustn't find them,' I protest. 'They just mustn't, Lawrie!'

He shrugs. 'They probably won't – I think they're safe enough, for now. But we can't keep them hidden forever, can we?'

'Not forever,' I agree. 'But I am working on a plan, don't worry. A way to get them out of there.'

'OK,' he says. 'But I'm worried about the dapple-grey mare. She's been neglected and she's quite run-down. She could be closer to foaling than we think.'

❀❀❀❀❀❀❀❀❀❀❀❀❀❀❀❀❀❀❀❀❀

'Don't worry about that,' I say briskly. 'I'm going to be a vet, remember? Delivering a foal would be no problem at all.'

I promise myself I'll find out on the Internet how to help a pony foal. I have watched a sheep give birth, on the farm next door to Tanglewood, but I'm not sure that makes me an expert in animal midwifery.

'Let's just hope she doesn't foal too soon,' Lawrie grumbles. 'She's not really strong enough yet and if we need veterinary help this whole kidnap thing could back-fire on us, big style.'

'It won't,' I say. 'Don't be so defeatist!'

Lawrie laughs, but there is no warmth, no humour in the sound of it.

'When are you going to learn, Coco?' he says with a sigh. 'Wake up, will you, and open your eyes. Not every-thing in life has a happy ending. Not everything that's broken can be fixed. What if we've made everything worse for Caramel and the mare? If they're found now they either go back to Seddon, or . . . they have no future at all.'

'What do you mean?'

'Think about it,' he says. 'What happens to ponies that can't be ridden, ponies that nobody wants? C'mon. You know all the answers, don't you?'

I shake my head, a feeling of dread inside me.

'They go to the knacker,' Lawries says flatly. 'They're put to sleep. Some of them even end up as *dog food*, OK? Or cheap burgers. Is that what you want for your precious Caramel?'

'No!' I whisper. 'No, of course not!'

I bite my lip until I can taste blood.

16

We stay up at Jasmine Cottage until past seven. We prop open the creaky back door of the cottage, allowing the ponies access to what was once a stone-floored kitchen. A couple of candle lanterns hang from the ceiling, giving out a thin, yellow light; an armchair with the springs and stuffing hanging out of it sits forlornly beside a rusted iron fireplace. If this place was Lawrie's summer hideout, he hasn't done much to make the place comfortable.

The two of us bicker endlessly over everything from names for the mare to how to provide the ponies with food. Lawrie wants to 'borrow' grain from the riding school, but that feels dishonest to me and neither of us has spare cash to pay. Both ponies have bridles and leading reins and Caramel has a saddle, but that's all we have – no grooming kit, no blankets to keep them warm and dry once the weather turns really cold.

My head is already working on ways to raise cash to cover the costs. It's time somebody took charge and got organized around here. I take out a notepad and begin making a list.

But Lawrie is right – if the mare foals early, we are in trouble. Big trouble . . .

By Tuesday night, the list has filled most of the notebook. I have packed a big travel bag with bright cushions, blankets and a few strings of solar-powered fairy lights – Mum and Paddy bought loads of them for the wedding party in June, and a whole bundle got boxed up and put away in the shed. I chuck in last year's fluffy boots, a pair of leggings and an old fisherman's sweater of Dad's I've had hidden at the back of my wardrobe ever since he left us.

It still smells of him, a little bit, and in a good way. There was a time when I used to snuggle up with it whenever I was sad because it made me think of Dad and fooled me into feeling he was still around, for a moment at least. These days I am much less easily fooled – it's just a ratty old jumper he used to wear when he worked in the garden, and it will keep me warm up at the derelict cottage.

I have packed a rucksack with biscuits and chocolate and apples, and after school tomorrow I will make a flask of hot chocolate to bring.

It looks a little like I am leaving home, but Mum and Paddy are too busy in the workshop to notice. Tanglewood is buzzing. Paddy's stable-block chocolate factory is working flat out, the B&B's breakfast room transformed into a packing room. At four o'clock the afternoon shift leaves and the evening shift arrives, and in the middle of it all Mum is making phone calls and signing for deliveries and making a tray of tea and biscuits for the workers. Paddy hasn't taken a break since breakfast time, but he can't stop grinning and his eyes shine like some modern-day Willie Wonka. This is his dream, his big chance to let The Chocolate Box grow into a well-known brand.

I am very happy for Mum and Paddy, but let's face it, Honey, Skye, Summer, Cherry and I could probably paint ourselves blue, dress in grass skirts and party until dawn with assorted wild boy-band lads right now, and they wouldn't even notice. Not that we'd want to, obviously. Or I wouldn't, anyhow. I am just glad that in all the madness nobody asks awkward questions about why I am taking bags of blankets and cushions out of the house.

I hide my supplies in the gypsy caravan, then head back to the kitchen and whisk up a double batch of cupcakes. I fill four trays and slide them into the oven, then rinse the mixing bowl and start work on a big carrot cake. If the ponies need cash for food, I will get it for them, and experience has taught me that cakes are the surest way to do it. Sarah, Amy and Jayde have promised to make traybakes and rocky road and scones for tomorrow too.

When the cupcakes are cool, I slice off the tops, scoop a little sponge out and spoon in thick, sweet caramel to create a cupcake version of Paddy's Coco Caramel truffles. I am pretty sure my secret ingredient will have the kids at school lining up for more, and surely it will bring luck to the real-life Caramel?

'What are the cakes for?' Skye queries, padding through to the kitchen to make hot chocolate. 'Giant panda? Siberian tiger? Blue whale?'

'Local pony sanctuary,' I lie, as confidently as I can. 'You probably won't have heard of it. But if you want to lend a hand . . .'

'Sure,' Skye shrugs. 'I'll rope in Summer and Cherry too!'

Skye and Cherry help me to ice the cupcakes with buttercream and piped horseshoe motifs. Summer whips up cream-cheese frosting for the carrot cake, not taking even the tiniest taste for herself. She loves to bake and cook, especially lately – she just doesn't eat any of what she makes, and she thinks we don't notice.

'How's the day clinic thing going?' I ask.

Summer blinks. 'It's OK, I suppose – I like the doctor running it. I just don't know if I need to be there. I know I was a little bit stressed a while back, but I'm fine now, really.'

'Eating normally?' I dare to ask, and Skye shoots me a warning glance.

'Well, not like before,' Summer admits. 'But normal for me now. The doctor says that something like this can't be fixed overnight, but . . . I put on another kilo this week – that's good, isn't it?'

'Brilliant,' I say, although to me Summer still looks almost as skinny and fragile as she did back in August. Still, at least she is eating with us these days, even if she has the kind of portions that would leave a mouse asking for more.

'Oh – I know someone whose little sister goes to the dance school in Minehead,' I say, thinking of Lawrie. 'She's eight. I don't know her name, though . . .'

'I probably know her,' Summer shrugs. 'I worked with a lot of the little ones at the summer dance classes. It's the best age, really. Everything seems so easy when you're eight . . .'

She looks wistful, thinking back to a time when Dad still lived here, when baking was all about scraping the mixing bowl clean and sampling the cakes while they were still warm from the oven. She wasn't scared of anything back then.

I hate the way things change.

While the twins pack the cakes into tins for me, Cherry helps me to chop up an old sheet (a new sheet, actually, but Mum will never notice) and paint *Exmoor Pony Sanctuary* on it in giant rainbow-coloured letters.

'Where's it based, this Exmoor Pony Sanctuary?' Skye asks, running a finger round the bowl that had held the buttercream icing and licking it before dumping the bowl into the sink. 'Is it new?'

'Quite new,' I say vaguely, exchanging glances with Cherry. 'It's up on the moors somewhere, I think. They're just a small set-up, but they do some amazing work, and they really need the money.'

'Good luck to them,' Summer says. 'They should be careful, though. My French teacher Miss Craven said two horses were stolen from a new trekking centre near Hartshill at the weekend. Some people will do anything for money!'

'A trekking centre?' Cherry asks, puzzled. 'I heard it was just a farm.'

'No, the horses were valuable, apparently,' Summer says. 'The owner is really upset. Who would steal animals, seriously?'

'No idea,' I say, but my voice seems to wobble as I speak. 'Awful.'

'By the way,' Skye chips in. 'Miss Craven gave me some worksheets for Honey too. She asked if she was feeling any better – I didn't know what to say. Something very dodgy is going on, I'm sure of it – no matter what Honey's school report says.'

Dismay curdles in my stomach, cold and uncomfortable. What is going on?

'She's skipping school again, or French lessons at least,' I say. 'Did you confront her?'

'She was on the bus as usual, so I just handed over the work,' Skye shrugged. 'I told her Miss Craven was asking after her. She laughed and said the teacher must be mixing her up with someone else. I don't believe her, though. That school report was perfect, but does Honey strike you as a reformed character?'

'No way,' Cherry says. 'Something fishy's going on.'

'Have the teachers said anything to you?' I ask.

My stepsister shrugs. 'Not exactly. But I did overhear a couple of them talking about Honey the other day. How she'd clearly given up, and how Dad and Charlotte don't seem to be bothered.'

'Not bothered?' I say, outraged. 'They've done everything possible to support Honey! And if her school report says everything is fine, then why should they be worried anyway?'

✿✿✿✿✿✿✿✿✿✿✿✿✿✿✿✿✿✿✿✿✿✿✿

Summer frowns. 'I don't know. Something's wrong, isn't it?'

'Definitely,' Skye agrees. 'I haven't seen Honey in school for ages. Should we say something? Forget that pact we made when we were little – some things shouldn't stay secret.'

Cherry shoots me a knowing look, and I avoid her gaze.

'We can't tell,' I argue. 'What would we say? After that report, it would just look like we were stirring up trouble.'

'But if we're right, and we don't speak out, isn't that worse?' Summer worries.

'Could we talk to Honey?' Cherry suggests sensibly. 'She's not going to listen to me, obviously, but perhaps one of you could speak to her?'

The twins exchange anxious looks.

'It'll look like we don't trust her,' Summer says.

'Like we're calling her a liar,' Skye echoes. 'Could you do it, Coco? You're the youngest, she won't get so cross with you.'

'Maybe,' I say, chewing my lip. 'If I get the chance . . .'

But digging up Honey's secrets is not top of my to-do

135

list right now; it would feel kind of hypocritical, when I am keeping so many of my own.

By midnight, I am alone in the kitchen. My sisters have gone to bed, the evening chocolate factory shift has long since finished and Mum and Paddy have headed upstairs with hot chocolates and bleary smiles. I am sitting at the kitchen table, a riot of felt pens all around me, drawing posters for the imaginary Exmoor Pony Sanctuary and eating one of the reject cupcakes, with Fred curled up at my feet, when the back door creaks open and Honey sneaks in. If she is startled to see me, she doesn't show it.

'Colouring in, little sister?' she asks, kicking her shoes off beside the door. 'Cute.'

'Fund-raising,' I correct her. 'How about you? Late night with the long division? Or was Anthony explaining some fascinating chemical equations? You're such a geek-girl these days, Honey. Not.'

'Funny,' she says. 'I *was* studying – sort of – to begin with, at least. But . . . not with Anthony.'

I sigh, taking in the slightly smudged lipstick, the rumpled hair. 'I don't think I'll ask *what* you were studying . . .'

'Don't,' Honey advises. 'And don't tell on me, OK?'

This is the perfect moment to challenge Honey about her school attendance, ask whether she's hiding something. Who knows, she might even tell me – but what then? I don't want to betray Honey's trust any more than I want Cherry to betray mine. Perhaps it's better not to know.

'I won't give you away,' I promise, although I think that someone probably needs to tell on Honey, for her own sake. And soon.

It just won't be me.

17

Some days I feel so full of energy I think I could conquer the world. My sisters would say it's sugar overload, but I disagree. I spring out of bed after just six hours' sleep, feeling like anything is possible; I have a list, I have cakes, I have bucketloads of determination – what's to stop me?

Mum and Paddy are sitting at the kitchen table eating porridge with raisins and cinnamon, and I help myself to a bowlful as I come in. My sisters are already there, talking about the bonfire party down in the village – Mum and Paddy are planning to work through the weekend, so we won't be having our usual beach bonfire party.

'I've been invited by some friends,' Honey says sweetly. 'If I'm allowed to go, that is? It's the girls from my lunchtime history club. We were going to look at the origins of Guy Fawkes night, have some food . . .'

Mum and Paddy exchange glances. 'Don't forget you're still grounded, Honey,' Mum points out. 'I know this is a study group, but . . .'

'Maybe we can bend the rules, just this once,' Paddy says. 'I think you should go, Honey. It sounds quite educational.'

It sounds quite unlikely to me, but who am I to say?

'Thank you, Paddy,' Honey says through gritted teeth.

'We're going to the village bonfire too,' Skye chips in. 'Want to tag along, Coco?'

That stings. Why am I never included properly? Why am I the tag-along, the one nobody ever takes seriously?

'I'm already going out,' I say coldly. 'With Jayde and Amy and Sarah. We are having an important fund-raising meeting for the pony sanctuary first, and planning a protest, because fireworks are actually quite distressing for pets, and there's really no need to have rockets and the ones that make those shrieking noises . . .'

'Saint Coco,' Honey says. 'Are you going to ban fun too?'

❀❀❀❀❀❀❀❀❀❀❀❀❀❀❀❀❀❀❀❀❀❀❀❀

I stick my tongue out at my big sister. I am about to tell her that Saturday is Sarah's birthday and that we are all going to the big firework display in Minehead and then on to the funfair, when there is a loud knock on the door. Paddy answers; there are two policemen on the doorstep.

I drop my spoon, splattering porridge all over my school trousers.

'Just a courtesy call, sir,' one of the officers says. 'We're asking locals to keep an eye out for any suspicious characters, especially where there are horses close by. We're investigating the theft of two ponies at the weekend, and it's possible there may be more incidents if the thieves are still in the area. We'll catch them, it's just a matter of time, but until we do . . .'

My face is so warm I am pretty sure you could toast a bagel on it, but Cherry is the only one looking at me. Her eyes are wide, terrified, as if she expects the policemen to snap handcuffs on me and bundle me into a nearby prison cell. I suppose it could happen.

'We'll let you know if we see or hear of anything unusual,' Paddy says. 'It's actually a very friendly community, so if anything happens we'll probably hear of it. We don't have horses ourselves, though – just ducks, a dog and a very badly behaved sheep . . .'

As he trails away into silence, Humbug the sheep trots in from outside and helps herself to a reject scone from last night that has found its way into Fred's feeding dish. The policemen laugh and ask us all to be vigilant, and then they're gone.

The five of us walk down to the village bus stop together, my sisters helping to carry the bags and tins of cupcakes and traybakes. My conquer-the-world feeling has evaporated, replaced by a heavy, guilty heart. It's not like I have actually done anything wrong, of course; not *morally* wrong. I am pretty sure any judge in the land would understand that.

Maybe.

'Will you visit me in prison?' I ask Cherry in a whisper.

'You betcha,' she says.

'Another cake sale?' Mr Wolfe asks at break, raising an eyebrow. 'That's the fourth one since September, Coco. First it was to save the tiger, then the elephant, then the giant panda . . . now you're raising cash for some local pony sanctuary? The dinner ladies have been complaining that nobody buys puddings on the days you sell cakes, and the food science department is grumbling about healthy eating. It's wonderful that you try so hard to help, but I would make this one the last cake sale for now if I were you. Mrs Gregg is not happy.'

Mrs Gregg is the head teacher, and she is actually never happy. As far as I can see, this has nothing to do with cakes and more to do with the stresses of running a large middle school, but I don't say this. Cakes make people happy, not unhappy – it's a well-known fact. As for healthy eating, surely a home-made caramel cupcake is better than the crisps, fizzy pop and chocolate bars on sale in the canteen vending machines? And the reason people don't buy school puddings is because they are always pure stodge, like treacle tart or bread-and-butter pudding or rhubarb pie, and come with generous helpings of lukewarm, lumpy custard. If I were the food science department, I would focus my attentions on the dinner ladies, seriously.

I am lucky that Mr Wolfe is so used to my animal charity fund-raising that he doesn't question the imaginary pony sanctuary, though.

❀❀❀❀❀❀❀❀❀❀❀❀❀❀❀❀❀❀❀❀❀❀❀

'I probably won't be doing too many more sales before Christmas,' I explain, waving politely at Lawrie who is glaring at me from across the lobby. 'It's just that there are so many endangered species out there – they need our help. And this time I wanted to raise money for a new pony sanctuary. It's important, Sir, life and death really . . .'

I look across the busy cake-sale queue for Lawrie, but he has vanished, taking his own personal raincloud with him. You'd think he would at least support the cause. I wrap a couple of the prettiest caramel cupcakes in foil to give to him later – why should his little sister miss out just because Lawrie is too sour and stingy to cough up his cash?

'Can I interest you in a cupcake, Sir?' I ask Mr Wolfe. 'Caramel Surprise. You won't regret it!'

'I probably will,' he sighs. 'I'll take one, though – and one for Mrs Gregg. It might sweeten her up, though I think she means it about the cake-sale ban, Coco. Time to give other kids and other charities a chance. OK?'

This seems a bit mean. I can't remember any other student fund-raising attempts, except for the time Summer

❀❀❀❀❀❀❀❀❀❀❀❀❀❀❀❀❀❀❀❀❀❀❀❀❀

and Skye did a sponsored three-legged day for Children in Need two years ago. You would think Mrs Gregg would be happy to have caring, charitable pupils raising funds and awareness in her school, but no, clearly not.

'OK,' I agree, my shoulders slumping. 'I guess. I don't suppose you can donate a horse blanket or a bale of hay to the sanctuary, can you? Or an unwanted saddle or curry comb?'

'Funnily enough, no,' Mr Wolfe says, paying for his cupcakes. 'Good luck, Coco.'

Sarah and I have almost sold out by the time the weaselly Year Six boy sidles up, offering five pence for a slightly lopsided piece of rocky road.

'No discounts,' Sarah tells him firmly. 'It's for charity.'

He prods it a few times until it cracks right down the middle. 'You'll have to sell it to me now,' he says. 'I've touched it. And besides, it's broken. You should give it to me for free.'

'Not a chance,' Sarah says. 'You broke it, now you'd better pay for it. Full price.'

'Can't,' the kid says, smirking. 'No money.'

This is the boy Lawrie found trying to steal crispy cakes

❀❀❀❀❀❀❀❀❀❀❀❀❀❀❀❀❀❀❀❀❀❀❀

from a Year Five girl, though I can't remember his name. His sticky little hand pushes down on the last remaining scone, reducing it to a mess of crumbs and jam. I start to get angry.

'This is a charity sale,' I point out. 'Where's your compassion?'

'Lost it,' the kid quips. 'Careless, me . . .'

'Just push off,' Sarah says crossly. 'Loser!'

I pick up the broken rocky road and hold it out to the Year Six boy. 'Want it?' I offer. 'You can have it, I guess. Why not?'

'Don't,' Sarah frowns. 'He doesn't deserve it.'

'Oh, but he does,' I say. 'He really, really does. What's your name, anyhow?'

The boy looks uncertain. 'Look,' he says, 'I don't really want your stupid cake. It was just a joke.'

'Your name?' I repeat, grabbing hold of his sleeve so he can't run away. 'Don't be shy, you can tell me.'

'Darren,' he mutters. 'Let me go!'

'You were the one who hoisted my panda hat up the school flagpole, weren't you?' I ask him. 'And the one who tried to steal a tin of crispy cakes from a Year Five

❀❀❀❀❀❀❀❀❀❀❀❀❀❀❀❀❀❀❀❀❀❀❀

kid, until Lawrie Marshall stopped you. I guess you deserve that cake because you're so *big* and so *brave*, right?'

I wave the rocky road slice in front of his nose, and he jerks his head away.

'Don't you want it any more?' I tease. 'You seemed so sure a minute ago. And it's not like we can sell it, not now you've put your sticky paws all over it.'

'Get off!' he snarls, and as he opens his mouth I shove a corner of cake in. It breaks and leaves a smear of chocolate across his face. He squirms away from me but I hang on to his sleeve, unshakeable. I may be smaller than this boy by a couple of inches, but I am stronger than I look.

'Not hungry?' I persist. 'Or have you changed your mind? Would you rather have a scone?'

'Gerroff me!' he yells. 'You've got the wrong person, OK? It was a misunderstanding. She offered me a crispy cake, and that Lawrie kid got the wrong idea. Mnnnnfff!'

I score a direct hit with the mashed-up scone. A shower of crumbs falls to the floor and Darren wipes his face, leaving a trail of strawberry jam across one cheek.

✿✿✿✿✿✿✿✿✿✿✿✿✿✿✿✿✿✿✿✿✿✿✿✿

'Leave the little kids alone from now on,' I tell him. 'Nobody likes a bully. OK?'

'OK . . .'

'Quick,' Sarah hisses. 'It's Wolfie!'

Mr Wolfe cuts his way through the crowd just as Darren ducks free at last, wriggling out of his blazer completely and leaving me holding the sleeve.

'Everything all right here?' the history teacher asks.

'Fine,' Darren splutters through a mouthful of cake. 'Mnnnfff. Perfect, Sir.'

'Coco?' Mr Wolfe presses. 'Darren not bothering you, is he?'

'Not at all,' I say sweetly, handing back the crumb-speckled blazer. 'Not at all.'

18

'Are you crazy?' Lawrie demands when I bring my bike to a wobbling halt beside the hazel trees at the moor's edge. 'You're taking all those bags up to the cottage? Seriously?'

I roll my eyes and refuse to answer.

'Are you moving in?' he goes on. 'Got your favourite knick-knacks and fluffy floor rugs? Did you pack a kitchen sink and a mattress, just in case? And more to the point, are you expecting me to help you carry all that junk?'

'No,' I tell him, wheeling my bicycle through the trees. 'Hoping, yes; expecting, no . . .'

'I worry about you,' Lawrie growls. 'We are in the middle of a very serious situation, and you spend your time carting great bags of stuff around and baking cupcakes for some imaginary pony sanctuary.'

I grit my teeth and fish out the cake-sale cash from my shoulder bag, stuffing it into Lawrie's pocket. 'Thirty-seven pounds, almost,' I tell him, 'The caramel cupcakes were a big hit. Enough to buy feed for the ponies for a week or two, anyway. Unless you already found the money some place else . . .'

'No,' Lawrie admits. 'Well, OK. That's good then. Thank you.'

'Hurt to say that, didn't it?' I ask.

'A bit,' he grins, and I think again that Lawrie could be a whole lot nicer to be around if he just smiled more.

He takes the bicycle handlebars from me and begins pushing slowly uphill. 'The easiest way to carry it is to leave it all strapped to the bike,' he says. 'I did it yesterday, bringing up more hay from the stables after work.'

'All I'm doing is trying to help too, you know,' I say.

'I know,' Lawrie admits. 'I suppose we just go about things differently. I've been trying to make the place a bit more liveable as well. And the money will be useful. I'm just worried about those ponies, that's all.'

'You and me both,' I tell him. 'The police came to our house this morning, warning us that horse thieves were in the area – I swear, I nearly fainted with terror. I didn't think they would actually make a big thing of it – I mean, it's not exactly a murder or a gang war, is it? I suppose that's what happens when you live in a place where nothing ever happens.'

'Maybe,' Lawrie says. 'Seddon was always going to make a fuss, that's just the kind of bloke he is. You don't make an enemy of a thug like him.'

'Well, I have,' I say briskly. 'And I don't care. Besides, I've been thinking about the ponies, and I reckon I've come up with a plan . . .'

I tell Lawrie my ideas as we hike upstream together in the fading light, the wind ruffling our hair and pinching our cheeks raw. With Caramel, the plan is simple; I want to keep her. If I really work on Mum and Paddy – and if the chocolate order comes good and the cash starts rolling in – there's a chance it could happen. I would just have to wait a while, then set up a fake ad for an easy-going bay pony. I could say I'd seen it on the riding school noticeboard – who would ever know? If the price was right, Mum might just go for it.

'Caramel's not exactly easy-going, though, is she?'

✿✿✿✿✿✿✿✿✿✿✿✿✿✿✿✿✿✿✿✿✿✿✿✿✿

Lawrie points out 'And your mum was dead against you buying her, so . . .'

'That's the point,' I explain. 'She won't know it's her – she's never actually met Caramel, only heard about her. We'll make up a new name – I was thinking maybe "Cupcake".'

'No surprises there,' Lawrie says.

'Then we invent a new history for her . . . reluctant sale, child's pony, now outgrown . . . needs loving home. Simple but brilliant!'

'I think you've forgotten something,' he says. 'Half of Somerset is looking for Caramel. You can't just move her into Tanglewood – people will put two and two together!'

'I don't think so,' I reply. 'Sometimes, the best place to hide something is in full view, right under everyone's noses. It's all about confidence. Nobody's going to expect her to turn up just down the road, and it's not as if Seddon knows my family or anything. The police were warning us to look out for thieves, not searching for missing horses. If we give Caramel a new identity, it'll stick, I'm sure of it!'

✿✿✿✿✿✿✿✿✿✿✿✿✿✿✿✿✿✿✿✿✿✿✿✿✿✿✿

'You're going to ask your mum to pay money for her?' Lawrie checks.

'Yes, it has to be plausible. If I was suggesting we take in a pony for free, that would be way more suspicious!'

'So . . . how do we arrange the actual sale?' he wants to know. 'Your mum will want to talk to Caramel's "old owners". She won't just give you the cash and wait for you to come home with a horse, will she? She'll want to meet the owners, do it properly.'

I adjust my rucksack, stopping for a moment to catch my breath. 'That's where you can help,' I tell him. 'Mum doesn't know you, or your family. I thought maybe you could get your mum or dad to pretend to be Caramel's owners?'

'You thought wrong,' Lawrie snaps. 'Forget it!'

We walk on in silence for a few moments, following the stream, and even in the dusk I can see Lawrie's lips are tight, his knuckles white on the bicycle handlebars. I know better than to argue – something has upset him, something I've said. Talking to him is like walking through a minefield – put the slightest foot wrong and everything blows up in your face.

❀❀❀❀❀❀❀❀❀❀❀❀❀❀❀❀❀❀❀❀❀❀❀

'Dad left us,' he says into the silence eventually. 'Couple of years ago. We haven't heard from him since – no phone calls, no maintenance, nothing. So no, I can't ask him to help out with your little scheme, Coco. And my mum can't help either, OK? She has enough problems of her own right now.'

'OK,' I tell him. 'I'm sorry.'

There is no sound except for our footfalls through the heather, the whirr of dynamo lights on my bike in the falling light.

'My dad left too,' I whisper. 'Sucks, right?'

'Just a bit.'

'Mine lives in Australia now,' I explain. 'Like London wasn't far enough – he had to go and move to the other side of the world. Makes you feel really wanted, y'know? Mum got married again in June, though, and I have a new stepdad now. Paddy – he's nice.'

I am surprised at how easy it is to say all this out loud – talking about Dad has always been off-limits for me, except with my sisters. Maybe it's the darkness closing around us, the cold wind, the fact that Lawrie's face is hidden beneath a fall of dark wavy hair, his eyes facing forward as he pushes the overloaded bike. Maybe it's because I think, crazy though it may seem, that the prickliest boy in the school might just understand.

Or not.

'Look, Coco, I can't talk about this,' he mutters. 'Not right now. I'm glad things are getting better for you, but – sheesh – what's in all these bags? Bricks?'

I roll my eyes. 'That's right. Thought we could rebuild the tumbledown walls and maybe install a ski-lift at the same time, make it easier to get up and down . . .'

'Ha,' he says. 'I knew you'd get fed up with it.'

'Did I complain?' I argue. 'I did not. But we both know this hiding place is only temporary – we need to move the ponies to safety. If we can't get any adults to pretend to be selling Caramel . . . OK, change of plan; you can pretend to be the son of the owners. Mum's never met you, so it could work.'

'She'll never take any notice of a kid!'

'Got a better idea?'

He sighs. 'OK. Supposing – just supposing – things work out with Caramel. What about the dapple-grey?'

'That's where it gets clever. We use the money from

✿✿✿✿✿✿✿✿✿✿✿✿✿✿✿✿✿✿✿✿✿✿✿✿✿✿

the "sale" of Caramel to hire a horsebox and driver and get her taken out of Somerset – to a real pony sanctuary. I've googled one in Wiltshire that takes in unwanted ponies and then rehomes them – they homecheck the new owners to be certain they're OK. Our grey could have her foal safely and then both she and the baby would have a fresh start, a new life. We'll have to invent a convincing backstory for her – perhaps say her owner died suddenly . . .'

'Do you think they'll take her?' Lawrie asks.

'No idea, but we have time to work on that, don't we?'

'Might work,' he concedes. 'As long as the sanctuary hasn't heard about the theft. At least you didn't suggest painting her brown and setting her loose on the moors.'

'That was my Plan B,' I grin. 'Let's hope it doesn't come to that. We'd have to use poster paint, and it rains a lot in Somerset . . .'

Images of a paint-streaked pony, rainbow-bright and round as a barrel, flash across my mind. I think Lawrie may be thinking something similar because he starts to grin, and by the time we reach the ruined cottage, the two of us are laughing.

✿✿✿✿✿✿✿✿✿✿✿✿✿✿✿✿✿✿✿✿✿✿✿✿

We work together in the twilight, feeding the ponies and grooming them as best we can. While I focus on Caramel, I notice that Lawrie is stroking the dapple-grey pony and feeding her grain from his palm . . . her trust is growing day by day, as if she knows that we mean her no harm.

'She's definitely not so frightened,' Lawrie says. 'Now that she's putting on a little weight, though, I'm sure she's nearer to foaling than we think.'

Disquiet settles inside me, and I shake it off, briskly.

'We need a name for her,' I say, changing the subject. 'We can't just keep calling her "the grey". Something positive, hopeful. Any ideas?'

'We'll never agree,' Lawrie says. 'Not a chance. You'll want to call her something sickly, like Sugar or . . . I dunno, Shortcake.'

'We'll pull names out of a hat,' I tell him. 'Compromise.'

'You? Compromise?' he teases. 'That'll be the day.'

An hour later, we are huddled in the kitchen drinking hot chocolate from the flask, a fire made of fallen branches roaring in the grate, candle lanterns that give out yellow pools of light hanging from the ceiling. A worn Indian rug covers the cold flagstones, cushions and blankets scattered across it. It's still cold because half the door is missing, and Caramel is leaning over what is left of it, her brown eyes glinting in the darkness.

'Any more suggestions?' I ask, scribbling names on scraps of paper and folding them before dropping them into the fluffy panda hat positioned between us.

'Shadow?' he offers. 'Misty? Swift? Whisper?'

'Good ones,' I say, scribbling them down and adding them to the lucky dip. 'OK. New name, new start . . . I'll mix them up and you pick.'

I stick my hand into the fun-fur hat to stir up the folded papers at exactly the same time as Lawrie goes to fish out a name, and both of us jump and mutter 'sorry' and pull our hands away as if we've been burnt.

Awkward.

'Did you pick?' I ask, watching him unfold his piece of paper.

'Spirit,' he reads. 'OK . . . that kind of suits her. Sorted then.'

Lawrie grins in the half-light, chinking his tin mug of hot chocolate against mine. 'So . . . do you want to come up on Saturday for a while?' he asks. 'If you're not busy, that is?'

'Don't you have to do something with your little sister?' I recall.

He shrugs. 'She has a ballet class at ten, but Mum can take her just this once. We could meet at ten or eleven, spend the whole day if you want to. It'd be nice to work with the ponies in daylight for a change. Or I could just come by myself . . .'

'No,' I tell him. 'I'll come. I have to go out later because it's Sarah's birthday and we're all going to the firework display in Minehead and on to the fair, but that won't be until evening, obviously, so I can still be here. Hey, I meant to ask, what's your sister's name? My big sister Summer goes to the dance school – she might know her. She often works with the little ones.'

'She hasn't been there long,' Lawrie says vaguely. 'She's not a great dancer, it's more a way of getting her out of the house, having her involved in something, y'know?'

I don't know, but Lawrie isn't giving any more away. His family, even his little sister, seems to be strictly off-limits. I fish the foil-wrapped cupcakes from earlier out of my rucksack. 'You didn't buy any cakes today, but I thought your little sister might like some anyway,' I tell him. 'I saved her some – you said she liked them.'

Lawrie smiles. 'She'll love them,' he says. 'Thanks, Coco. What is it with girls and cake?'

'True love,' I tell him. 'Cake never lets you down.'

19

I've been dreading Friday's riding lesson. I'm worried that everyone will be talking about the pony rustlers and that I'll somehow give myself away – and I haven't managed to apologize yet about riding Caramel without permission.

Besides, I'd much rather be up on the moors with Caramel and Spirit.

As predicted, my lesson is not the same without Caramel. An hour of hacking through the woods on Bailey with Kelly telling me about 'poor Mr Seddon' just about kills me. 'He won't let a bunch of horse thieves stop him,' Kelly insists. 'He wants to open a trekking centre – Jean and Roy reckon he's been asking around, trying to get new ponies. I think they're sorry they sold him Caramel now, what with the horse thieves and everything. And it's a bit cheeky to start up a trekking business so close to the stables. It would take custom from Jean and Roy, wouldn't it? Still, I do feel sorry for Seddon, losing two lovely horses to lowlife thieves . . .'

I open my mouth to tell Kelly exactly what I think of Seddon, then close it again. I would only incriminate myself. I realize then that no matter what Lawrie and I have done to get Caramel and Spirit to safety, we can't stop Seddon – he has money, status, power. It is all very depressing.

'I don't think I can face any more riding lessons right now,' I tell Lawrie afterwards, leading Bailey back to his stable. 'It's all spoilt. I don't want to be here now that Caramel's gone, and if Kelly tells me one more time what a shame it is for that rat Seddon I might lose the plot and tell her what a loser he really is.'

'Don't do that,' he says, lifting Bailey's saddle off and brushing him down. 'She'll start to wonder why you think so, and there's no way you can tell her without setting off alarm bells. Seddon's respected around here – nobody'd believe you, and it'd put the ponies in danger.'

I sigh. 'Well, if I stick around here I will put my foot in it for sure. I love riding, obviously, but . . . I think I'll take a break from lessons for now. Caramel and Spirit need me.'

'What will you tell your parents?' Lawrie asks. 'If you just stop, it might look suspicious!'

I shrug. 'I won't tell them. I'll find something else to do on Fridays – the school orchestra practise that day and Miss Noble is running auditions for new members. Paddy's taught me a few tunes and I practise every day, so they'd probably snap me up.'

'Modest, aren't you?' Lawrie asks.

'Just confident,' I shrug. 'And hopeful.'

Lawrie rolls his eyes. 'It's like you just naturally expect things to work out for you. As if you can pass every exam, get to uni, be a vet or whatever it is you want to do and then play in some orchestra in your spare time . . .'

'Don't forget about saving the whale, the tiger and the giant panda,' I grin. 'And setting up my own animal sanctuary. You've got to dream, haven't you? And it's no fun at all unless you believe that you can make it happen. It's hardly going to happen if you *don't* believe it, is it?'

'You make it sound so easy!'

❀❀❀❀❀❀❀❀❀❀❀❀❀❀❀❀❀❀❀❀❀❀❀

'Not easy, exactly, but . . . well, I don't see why it can't happen. Some of it, anyway. What about you? What would you like to be doing in ten years' time?'

'I'll still be shovelling wet straw, cleaning out stables,' Lawrie says gloomily. 'Not that I mind, exactly – I love working with horses. But I'm not like you, Coco. School stuff isn't easy for me.'

'It isn't easy for anyone, you just have to be organized and put in the work –'

'Not that simple,' he interrupts. 'Trust me.'

'But –'

'But nothing, OK? Just leave it!'

Lawrie ruffles Bailey's mane and walks out of the stable, leaving me pink-cheeked and open-mouthed. I hate the way that boy can switch from friendly to furious in the blink of an eye.

Some people are just plain impossible.

With ponies, you have to be patient, gentle, kind. You need to build up a trust. It's the same with any animal, really – Grandma Kate once had an old rescue dog called Gigi who would growl like crazy if you ever tried to take

❀❀❀❀❀❀❀❀❀❀❀❀❀❀❀❀❀❀❀❀❀❀❀❀

anything away from her. I found that out the hard way on one visit – Gigi had run off with one of my new red sandals and was trying to shred it, and I yelled and made a grab for it and ended up with grazed knuckles where she'd snapped at me.

Grandma Kate explained that rescue dogs have had a tough past, coping with things we can barely imagine – Gigi had been abandoned and lived on the streets for months, foraging and fighting for food. That was why she was so possessive about things now. Grandma Kate showed me how to talk softly to Gigi, calming her, stroking her, and when I finally took the chewed-up sandal away she barely even noticed. Minutes later, the grumpy old mongrel was rolling on her back, sighing with contentment while I tickled her tummy and scratched her ears. It was like being given a secret – instead of reacting with anger or exasperation, show animals kindness and most of the time they will do pretty much anything you want.

Lawrie's approach to the ponies is the same; he is calm, firm, gentle. It's like watching a completely different boy from the mean, moody middle-school version. Animals bring out the best in him, I can see that.

❀ ❀

I wonder if the calm, gentle approach works with people too?

I have already decided to tame Lawrie Marshall with smiles and kind words, but progress is painfully slow. He is worse than Spirit – he edges towards friendliness, then backs away, bucking and rearing. Well, not actually bucking and rearing, but you know what I mean. He is wild and angry and totally closed off.

If he were a pony I would offer him food, stroke his ears and scratch his neck; but he curls his lip at the idea of cake and I am seriously not going to stroke him. That would be just gross.

In spite of it all, the two of us have found a way to work together. By Saturday afternoon, Jasmine Cottage is starting to feel less like a ruin in the middle of nowhere and more like a den, a hideout. We've hauled more firewood into the murky kitchen, hung up extra lanterns and covered the wrecked armchair with an old quilt so it looks almost inviting, even if it is still wobbly to sit on. Outside, we have draped solar lights around the bushes to help when we're up there after dark and cleared the path that winds through the overgrown garden to the broken-down front door.

❀❀❀❀❀❀❀❀❀❀❀❀❀❀❀❀❀❀❀❀❀❀❀

'It's a bit of a giveaway if the police come looking,' Lawrie frowns. 'You may not be able to see anything from the moors, but once they're inside the gate they'd suss something was up.'

'If they came through the gate the ponies would definitely give the game away,' I point out. 'They're much less jumpy now. Caramel's really relaxed and even Spirit is much less shy than she was – the minute they hear the gate creak they trot over, looking for a treat or a cuddle. Face it, if the police find Jasmine Cottage, we've had it – we just have to hope they won't look here.'

'They won't,' he says firmly. 'I hope.'

As if on cue, Spirit appears, nudging me, looking for carrots and hugs. In just a couple of days she has transformed from a nervous, neglected mare into a bright-eyed pony with tons of personality. This morning I groomed and petted her while Lawrie mixed up the feed, and if I wasn't already in love with Caramel I am pretty sure I'd be falling for Spirit.

'She's much calmer,' Lawrie comments. 'It's like she's shrugging off the past six weeks, letting go of it all.'

❀❀❀❀❀❀❀❀❀❀❀❀❀❀❀❀❀❀❀❀❀❀❀❀

'Six weeks?' I question. 'Is that how long Seddon had her? How d'you know?'

He shrugs. 'I don't, obviously,' he says gruffly. 'Just guessing. What I mean is, she seems to have a good, steady temperament in spite of what she's been through, and she's young enough to learn to trust again. If we can just get her to that rescue place you talked about before she foals . . .'

'Not such a crazy idea after all then?'

'Sometimes the crazy ideas are the best,' he says.

'OK, so here's another – can I ride Caramel?' I ask, an arm slung around her neck, my face pressed against hers. 'Outside the garden, I mean? On the moors? Would it be safe?'

Lawrie frowns. 'It's just the risk of somebody seeing, but the moors really do seem deserted today . . .'

'So . . . ?'

He pulls a face. 'Knowing you, you'll do something stupid and she'll throw you, and I'll have to leg it to the road and flag down a passing ambulance.'

'Funny,' I say. 'I am pretty sure it was the scissors exercise that spooked her that day, and Kelly told me the last

❀❀❀❀❀❀❀❀❀❀❀❀❀❀❀❀❀❀❀❀❀❀❀❀

time Caramel reared the rider had been waving – she gets scared by anything happening behind her head. Maybe she's been hit or startled by something coming at her from behind?'

Lawrie narrows his eyes. 'I think you might be right,' he says. 'In any case, I think that with time and understanding she will overcome her fears. She just needs to learn to trust.'

'Like Spirit,' I say.

Like all of us, really, I think. *Lawrie, Honey, Summer . . . maybe even me.*

'I won't do anything to spook her,' I promise. 'I just think she needs the run.'

Lawrie shrugs. 'Well . . . up here I reckon we'd see people coming from miles away. I'll turn Spirit loose in the walled field, it'll do her good. Yeah . . . let's give it a try.'

I saddle Caramel, mount and ride her out along the crooked path and through the rickety iron gate. Starry white jasmine brushes my hair as I duck through, Lawrie leading Spirit behind me. He unlatches the gate of the enclosed field and lets the grey mare free. She hesitates for a moment, as if it's been way too long since she's had a taste of freedom, then begins to prance and play, finally bursting into a trot, her mane and tail flying.

'Will she come back, d'you think?' I ask.

'I reckon so,' Lawrie says. 'The field's all walled in, and she's getting to know us now. She'll come back, don't worry.'

I scan the moors around me, a patchwork of rough grass, purple heather and rust-brown bracken. Far below us in the distance the road snakes through the landscape, a dull grey thread occasionally brightened by the buzz of a car. There are no walkers, no birdwatchers, no tourists at all to worry about. Apart from a couple of rabbits mooching about in the distance, I cannot see another living creature anywhere. It feels like being on top of the world.

Caramel shakes her head, nostrils flared, and a shiver of excitement runs through her body. This is her habitat, her element; she fits into the wild landscape as if she was born to be here.

'Careful,' Lawrie tells me. 'Go easy. No riding hat and all that . . .'

'What are you, my mother?' I ask. 'I'll be fine.'

❀❀❀❀❀❀❀❀❀❀❀❀❀❀❀❀❀❀❀❀❀❀❀❀

'Sure. But Caramel can be a handful, you know that. Keep it slow, remember what happened last time.'

'Who's doing this?' I challenge, irritated. 'You or me?'

'There's no telling some people,' Lawrie grumbles, and before I can work out what he's doing, he takes Caramel's halter, leads her over to the field wall, clambers up over the mossy stones and slides into the saddle behind me. His arms close round me, warm hands covering mine, gathering up the reins.

'Lawrie, what the –'

My protests are lost in the wind as Caramel bursts forward into a trot, and as I struggle to adjust she moves seamlessly into a canter that lifts my hair and blows it back into his face.

'I don't need you or anyone else looking out for me,' I argue, but my protests are lost on the wind. 'I'm not some little kid, I –'

I swallow my words abruptly as Caramel lunges into a gallop that takes the breath from my body. I have never actually progressed as far as galloping, and suddenly I am terrified, clinging on for dear life.

'Relax,' Lawrie says into my ear. 'Let yourself be part

of the movement – lift yourself up out of the saddle, stand up in the stirrups . . .'

As I rise up in the stirrups, shakily, I am aware of Lawrie's body behind me, lean and muscled, and I can feel his warm breath against my neck, the roughness of the green Aran sweater he's wearing. Slowly, fear turns into exhilaration and I surrender to the hammering of my heart, the thud of hoofbeats on moorland. I have never felt so alive, not ever.

Moments later, Caramel slows again to a canter, then a trot and finally a walk, and I allow myself to slump back against Lawrie. I can feel the thumping of his heart as clearly as I can feel my own.

'What did you do that for?' I gasp, as soon as I can speak again. 'I thought you told me to go easy?'

'She wanted to gallop,' he says into my hair. 'I could have stopped her, but she's been cooped up all week – like you said, she needed the run. I didn't mean to scare you – you should have told me you'd never galloped before!'

'I have!' I scoff, but I'm not sure who I'm fooling. 'I've done it loads of times.'

❀❀❀❀❀❀❀❀❀❀❀❀❀❀❀❀❀❀❀❀❀❀❀

Except that I haven't, and I am pretty sure it was obvious. As for riding double with a boy, I have never done that, never even dreamt of it. I want to be angry, want to lash out and yell at Lawrie for treating me like a child, but I don't feel like a child right now. I am flushed and breathless and I like the feeling of a boy's arms wrapped round me, holding me close.

'She coped great,' Lawrie is saying. 'A flighty horse would have put her ears back and tried to throw us off, but Caramel took it all in her stride.'

'We weren't too heavy for her?' I ask.

'Doubt it. Neither of us weighs much – you're just a titch, and Exmoors were used as pit ponies once, y'know. She wouldn't have galloped like that if she'd been unhappy.'

Back at the cottage gate, we dismount awkwardly, suddenly shy. I lead Caramel forward and Lawrie calls Spirit over; she comes to him quietly, curious yet calm, as if she's known him forever. I watch him take her halter and realize that whatever his connection with animals, it goes way beyond being gentle and patient. He has something special, something magical.

172

Back inside the walled garden we unsaddle Caramel and set her loose, then sit for a moment in the crisp afternoon sunshine sharing apples and chocolate bars; as far as my theories on training go, this is kind of like offering grain to the ponies. Lawric eats and smiles and pushes a tangle of hair out of his eyes, but I cannot tell any more who is taming who.

Everything is the same as it was before, the garden cold and sunny and still, the scent of late jasmine drifting on the air, the cry of a buzzard circling overhead; but somehow, for me, everything is different.

20

I am baffled; I don't know what to make of Lawrie Marshall at all. One minute he is sour and moody, a scowling boy with an attitude problem the size of Exmoor; the next he is a hero, standing up for a bullied kid, taming two nervous, ill-treated horses, vaulting up into the saddle behind me to hold me tight as we gallop across the moors.

Sarah, Jayde and Amy would have a field day if they knew that last bit, but I am not about to tell them. I would never hear the last of it.

I pitch up at Sarah's house at six with a birthday card and prezzie, a fluffy tiger toy which is very cute and also very cool because when you buy it £2 gets donated to a tiger charity. The others are already there, eating pizza slices as they get ready for the firework display. Sarah

❀❀❀❀❀❀❀❀❀❀❀❀❀❀❀❀❀❀❀❀❀❀❀

seems to like my prezzie, but I can't help noticing that once she's thanked me she leaves it in a corner and goes back to experimenting with the glittery nail polishes and shimmery eye colours Jayde and Amy have given her.

It is very strange; Sarah never used to be a glittery kind of girl. She used to say that make-up was silly and pointless, but now she is giggling and posing in front of a mirror and trying on different combinations of clothes to wear to the firework display. I do not like the way growing up seems to be brainwashing my friends, wiping away their interests and turning them all into giggling boy-mad fashionistas.

'So, are we going to make some placards to take to the firework display?' I ask, trying to drag my friends away from the make-up. 'I thought we could campaign to end the sale of fireworks except for use in big displays . . . kids like that awful Darren are fiddling about with rockets and screamers for weeks in the run-up to November the fifth. Most pets get really freaked out by it all!'

Sarah, Amy and Jayde exchange glances.

'Is there any point?' Amy asks. 'It's a public firework display anyway. It's the shops that sell fireworks to the

✿✿✿✿✿✿✿✿✿✿✿✿✿✿✿✿✿✿✿✿✿✿✿

public you should be talking to, Coco. Or you could just leave it, try enjoying yourself instead. Why does everything have to be some kind of campaign?'

'It's Sarah's birthday,' Jayde reminds me. 'Let's just have fun!'

I sigh. There is only so long you can go on trying to change the world when nobody else is interested. It is a big task for just one person, and my friends seem to have switched allegiance lately. They still care about animals, I know – they just find other things much more pressing.

I bite into a slice of pizza and try not to wish I'd stayed up at the ruined cottage with Lawrie.

'Aren't you going to change, Coco?' Amy wants to know. 'I brought a couple of different skirts along if you want to borrow something, and Sarah's got a sparkly top that would really suit you.'

'I'm not wearing a skirt to a firework display,' I grumble. 'It's freezing! I've wrapped up warm specially, and besides, these are my best jeans!'

'You are such a tomboy,' Jayde says disapprovingly. 'Will you let me do your make-up? You could look *so*

❀❀❀❀❀❀❀❀❀❀❀❀❀❀❀❀❀❀❀❀❀❀❀❀❀

much more grown-up if you just used the teeniest bit of eyeliner and shadow . . .'

'I don't want to look grown-up,' I huff. 'I like looking like *me*!'

After an hour of fussing about in Sarah's bedroom, we escape out into the darkness, making our way down to the seafront where the firework display will be held. I have managed to escape unscathed apart from a slick of lipgloss and a little glitter across my cheekbones, but even so I am glad it is dark; I feel awkward, over-decorated, like one of those OTT houses all decked out in cheesy Christmas decorations that fascinate and appal at the same time.

The fireworks begin as we make our way across the beach, feet sinking into the gritty sand. We buy hot soup and huddle together as plume after plume of rainbow colour unfurls across the dark sky, squealing and laughing as the fireworks shoot and soar and shatter into tiny sparks and shards.

Fireworks are exciting, exhilarating; they wake you up, make your heart thump, shock and scare you with their drama, their chaos, their spectacle. There is a point where you have to give in, stop wishing you had a placard to wave and start letting yourself feel the celebration.

'Fun?' Sarah asks, linking my arm with hers as the explosive finale dies away. 'I know you don't really approve, but . . .'

'I loved it,' I tell her. 'Sorry if I was a bit grumpy earlier – I get a bit obsessed sometimes. It's just that I have a lot on my mind right now.'

'The horses?' she checks. 'I am so proud of you for rescuing them, Coco, I hope you know that. It's like you are actually doing things, changing things, when the rest of us just think about it – you're so brave!'

'I don't know about that . . .'

Any chance of a heart-to-heart evaporates as Jayde and Amy appear, herding us off towards the funfair. Open all season for tourists and holidaymakers, the fair traditionally closes down for the winter after the bonfire night display, so it's a last chance to celebrate, a perfect way to make the bonfire night fun stretch a little further.

We follow the crowds along the seafront towards the bright flashing lights and the smell of hot doughnuts and toffee apples, the loud music of the fair. It's ages since I've been, but I'm still a sucker for the thrill of it, the squash of people, the sense that something special is happening. I remember coming here when I was little with Mum and Dad, throwing ping-pong balls into glass bowls to win a teddy bear, getting candyfloss stuck to my face, flying round and round on the carousel horses and wishing they were real. More recently I've been with Mum and Paddy, or with Sarah's parents, but I have never been without a watchful adult hovering in the background.

An extra prickle of excitement slides down my spine.

'Let's go on the waltzers,' Amy is saying, tugging us forward. 'You should see the boys that work on it – they are so fit!'

'I think I just saw Aaron Jones from the high school,' Jayde chips in. 'Didn't he go out with Summer for a while? Maybe we should say hello?'

'Don't bother,' I say. 'He was a loser. A creep.'

'Good-looking, though,' Amy comments. 'Just wait till you see this lad at the waltzers! If he still works there . . . there are two of them, and the one I like is just soooo cool. Wait till you see!'

I roll my eyes and allow myself to be led through the

❀❀❀❀❀❀❀❀❀❀❀❀❀❀❀❀❀❀❀❀❀❀

knots of people to the waltzers, just in time to join the end of the queue as the ride comes to an end. One of the fairground workers is taking the money, another working on the ride itself, swinging back the safety bars and helping people out.

'That's him!' she whispers, breathless and pink-cheeked. 'Isn't he A-mazing?'

The legendary fairground boy is skinny and tanned with laughing eyes and darkly inked tattoos peeking out from the cuffs of his leather jacket. He's much older than us, and there's a rough edge to him that has my friends swooning.

He spots us waiting and waves us over to an empty waltzer, settles us in and pulls down the safety bar. 'Ready for the time of your life, girls?' he asks, confident and flirty. 'I'll make sure you have a good time!'

'He is SO good-looking!' Jayde whispers as soon as he moves on to the next waltzer. 'Like someone from a movie . . .'

'Way too old for us,' I point out. 'He must be at least seventeen or eighteen.'

'So what?' Amy shrugs. 'I'm not going to marry him, am I?'

❀❀❀❀❀❀❀❀❀❀❀❀❀❀❀❀❀❀❀❀❀❀

'Did you see his tattoos?' Sarah giggles.

'I saw him without his leather jacket, in the summer,' Amy says. 'The tattoos go right up his arms. Just imagine those arms round you!'

'Fairground boys are bad boys,' Jayde chips in. 'They smoke, they drink, they swear . . .'

'Who cares?' Amy giggles. 'They *flirt* as well!'

The music begins to build up again and the floor sways beneath us, the brightly painted waltzer car swaying with it. Squashed in between my friends, I hang on to the safety bar as we whirl round, slowly at first, then faster, faster. I am deafened by the music, the crash of the waltzers as they plunge and thunder round and round, clattering across the undulating floor, screams of laughter from all around us.

'All right, girls?' Tattoo Boy asks, stepping on to the back of our waltzer. 'Fast enough for you? Or would you like to see some real action?'

Laughing, he spins the waltzer round and all four of us yell like crazy, loving it, hating it, high as the moon. And then before we know it the ride is slowing, the music fading, the waltzers lurching to a halt.

❀❀❀❀❀❀❀❀❀❀❀❀❀❀❀❀❀❀❀❀❀❀❀❀

'There you go, sweethearts,' Tattoo Boy says, releasing the safety bar and setting us free. 'Come back again if you're after more thrills, OK?'

'We will!' Amy promises.

'Everything's spinning,' I complain, getting to my feet and flopping right back down again. 'Whoa!'

'I'm all dizzy,' Jayde yelps. 'I don't know if it was the ride or the flirting . . .'

'Fairground boys are mad, bad and dangerous to know,' Sarah proclaims as we cling together, making our way slowly across the undulating wooden floor. 'This has been the best birthday ever!'

We're staggering down the steps, still a little seasick from the ride, when Jayde tugs my sleeve. 'Hey, Coco,' she says. 'Isn't that your sister?'

I follow her gaze to where Tattoo Boy is leaning on the painted railings that edge the ride, talking to a pretty girl with jaw-length blonde waves, a green crochet hat, a wool jacket and the shortest skirt I have seen in quite some time.

My heart thumps.

'Honey?' I frown, shaking off my friends and running forward. 'Honey? What are you doing here?'

She looks at me, her gaze registering annoyance, then resignation, while Tattoo Boy watches, amused.

'I could ask you the same thing,' she snaps.

'It's Sarah's birthday, remember?' I say. 'We went to the firework display, then on here. Mum knows all about it.'

'Good for her,' Honey says, without missing a beat. 'Well, I'm at history club, remember? I am with the girls . . .'

She gestures towards a couple of hard-faced teenage girls in tight jeans and spike-heeled boots, leaning against the railing sharing a cigarette. They don't look like school-girls, or history geeks for that matter.

Tattoo Boy gives me an appraising look, then turns back to Honey. 'See you later,' he says, and goes back to the waltzers.

'What does he mean, "see you later"?' I demand. 'Don't tell me he's in your history club too? I may only be twelve years old, Honey, but I am not stupid!'

Honey rolls her eyes. 'OK, OK, I'll come clean,' she says. 'But you have to stay quiet about it, Coco, yeah? Because I am supposed to be grounded, as you know,

❁❁❁❁❁❁❁❁❁❁❁❁❁❁❁❁❁❁❁❁❁❁❁

and Mum and Paddy would go nuts if they knew I was
here. But it's not what you think. I am working on a
project for school . . .'

I blink. 'What project?'

Honey pulls a little camera from her pocket, pressing
the buttons to display past photographs.

'It's for my art portfolio,' she explains. 'I've been studying the fairground. I didn't think Mum would understand, but art is actually the only subject I really care
about and I want my portfolio to be as good as I can
make it.'

She flicks through some of the images; there are grainy
shots of Tattoo Boy leaning up against the painted fairground backboards, of the hard-faced girls, the man
taking the money, of little kids laughing as they queue at
the hot dog stand. They are good, as far as I can tell,
and relief floods through me.

'You see?' Honey says. 'It's an art project – I'm
researching for a painting. Nothing to worry about, and
no need to say anything to Mum and Paddy, right? They
might not understand, but you will, Coco, I know. I may
be grounded, but I don't want my art project to suffer.'

'I guess not . . .'

Honey hugs me, tousling my hair beneath the panda hat, and I run off to rejoin Sarah and the others.

I believe Honey – we all know how much she loves art – but I can't help feeling uneasy, all the same.

p.100

EXMOOR GAZETTE

REWARD OFFERED
FOR STOLEN PONIES

OWNERS URGED TO BE VIGILANT

21

I take a leaf out of Lawrie's book and start bringing my school work up to the cottage; now we curl up with our homework most afternoons. Lawrie turns out to be smarter than he thinks; he helps me with maths and CDT and I help him with English and French. It works both ways and it makes the homework fun.

I wonder if that's why Honey likes studying with Anthony? If she actually does study, that is. She can pick his brain and pull her grades up, and he can hang out with the girl he's had a crush on since forever. There is no crushing going on between Lawrie and me, obviously, although sometimes I catch him watching me in a way that makes my cheeks burn. It's probably just my own stupid imagination; as far as I can tell, Lawrie finds me every bit as exasperating as he always did. He is just getting better at hiding it.

Sometimes, anyway.

'This is just about the only time I get for homework lately,' I say, writing out maths problems by lantern light. 'I'm always up here, and things are kind of crazy at home just now because of the big chocolate order. How do you manage, with this and your job at the stables?'

'I don't,' Lawrie says, glancing up from an English essay. 'Not usually. I haven't handed in a piece of home-work on time for ages – Mr Wolfe almost fainted yesterday when I handed in that history assignment.'

'How come you got the stables job, anyway?' I press. 'I wanted to try out for it and they said I was too young, but you're twelve too, right?'

'I told them I was fourteen,' he shrugs. 'I needed the money.'

'How come?'

'Never mind,' he says.

'So . . . how come you don't study at home?' I ask.

'I just don't,' he says. 'You don't know what it's like at home for me. I'm too busy to study. Other things to do.'

❀❀❀❀❀❀❀❀❀❀❀❀❀❀❀❀❀❀❀❀❀❀❀❀

Lawrie is sending me back-off messages, loud and clear, but right now I don't want to take the hint.

'Like what?' I ask.

'Like looking out for my mum and my sister, helping around the place, that sort of stuff,' he growls. 'You're very nosy, aren't you?'

'You're very secretive,' I counter. 'What are you, some kind of pre-teen spy? You don't make it easy for anyone to get to know you.'

'Good,' Lawrie says. 'I'm not looking for friends. I had them once and I had to leave them all behind, so what's the point in making more? I hate it here. Move to the country, start over, Mum said – it's been a disaster from start to finish.'

I watch him in the half-light, leaning back against the broken-down armchair, his face unreadable. It's like he has forgotten I'm here.

'The only good thing about the countryside is the animals,' he goes on, gruffly. 'The people are rotten. They pretend to care, but they just gossip and gawp and never actually do anything at all, and the bullies get to call all the shots. How come some people think they can do whatever they want, treat everyone around them like dirt? There's no way out, and you can't even help the people you care about. I hate it!'

I blink. I have no idea what Lawrie is talking about, but it seems like more than just Darren Holmes nicking crispy cakes outside the school.

'Lawrie?' I whisper. 'I don't know what's going on, but if you ever want to talk –'

'I don't,' he snaps, jumping up, moving away into the shadows. 'I don't want to talk, not to you, not to anyone. Back off, Coco, OK? I am not one of your charity projects. Like I said, you can't fix everything that's broken – let go of it and leave me alone!'

Lawrie shoves his way out of the kitchen, but not before I see the glint of tears on his cheeks in the flickering lamplight. That shocks me more than anything because boys like Lawrie just don't cry.

It takes him half an hour to calm down, half an hour of clattering about in the dark, filling buckets with fresh water from the stream, chopping back overgrown branches with a pair of secateurs. Well, at least he doesn't storm off down to the road without me.

❀❀❀❀❀❀❀❀❀❀❀❀❀❀❀❀❀❀❀❀❀❀❀❀

I stay put, ploughing through my maths homework, hoping that if I am patient he will cool off and bluff his way forward as though the outburst never happened. 'Least said, soonest mended,' Grandma Kate used to say, and it's good advice. I have learnt the hard way that with a boy like Lawrie, patience heals a whole lot faster than panic ever can.

'You coming then?' Lawrie asks a while later. 'It's getting late; they'll be sending out a search party for you.'

'Some people will do anything to get out of doing an English essay,' I quip, packing up my rucksack. 'Moonlit gardening, huh?'

'Don't recommend it,' he says. 'I almost pruned Caramel in the dark there. She could have ended up with a topiary tail . . .'

We walk down across the moors in silence, but when we reach the hazel copse Lawrie turns to me, his face shadowed beneath the bare tree branches.

'I don't understand you,' he says. 'I don't understand why you stick around. You keep coming back, keep asking awkward questions and making me say stuff I really don't want to talk about. You drive me nuts and I think I drive you nuts too, but . . .'

His breath huffs out in a cloud of white, hovering in the icy air, and his brows draw together in a frown. 'I just don't get it!'

I sigh, wheeling my bike out on to the lane, hook a foot over one pedal.

'We're friends,' I tell him, pushing off into the darkness.

I think it's true.

At school, Lawrie mostly acts as though I don't exist, though if I pass him in the corridor or see him in the lunch hall he drags up a grudging 'hello'. He is a loner, dark wavy hair falling across his face, mouth unsmiling, blue eyes guarded. Sometimes I think he'd like to be invisible, but he's not, not to me.

On Thursday morning, Sarah, Jayde and Amy corner me at break.

'Did you see the newspaper?' Sarah asks, spreading a copy of the *Exmoor Gazette* out across the table. 'There's a big piece about the missing ponies. You're famous! Or infamous, maybe . . .'

'Shhh!' I hiss. 'Keep your voice down!'

I look at the headline – *Reward Offered for Stolen Ponies: Horse Owners Urged to be Vigilant* – and my heart begins to pound.

'*Ten days ago near Hartshill, heartless thieves stole a small girl's birthday pony, leaving her inconsolable,*' I read out. '*The much-loved family pet was taken, along with another valuable trekking pony in foal, in a well-planned midnight raid. Local landowner James Seddon is offering a cash reward for information leading to the return of the horses, and police fear the thugs may strike again . . .*'

'Are you sure they were being ill-treated?' Amy asks.

'Of course I'm sure!' I splutter. 'That article is rubbish! Trekking ponies? Spirit's only half-broken, and she was so petrified when we – I – first took her that I didn't think she'd ever calm down. And it's a miracle she is still in foal, after the way she's been neglected. As for the little girl, she looked as scared of Seddon as the ponies were. Honestly, I wish the newspaper knew what was really going on.'

'Offering a reward is bad news,' Jayde points out. 'People will be watching out for those ponies now. You shouldn't trust anyone.'

❀❀❀❀❀❀❀❀❀❀❀❀❀❀❀❀❀❀❀❀❀❀❀

'Especially not Jayde,' Amy grins, nudging her friend with an elbow. 'She talks too much. Walls have ears, right?'

'Huh?' Jayde asks. 'What walls? What are you talking about?'

'She's telling you to keep your voice down,' Sarah says, stuffing the paper into my schoolbag before anyone can see what we were reading, and glancing around furtively. 'We have to be extra careful now. Coco, are the . . . um . . . refugees definitely in a safe place?'

I blink. '*Refugees?*'

Sarah lowers her voice. 'You know what I mean! I don't want to say the word "horse". People might be listening!'

'Nobody's listening,' I tell her. 'I think they're safe, but . . . well, it's impossible to be sure, isn't it?'

'Better step up security then,' Sarah warns. 'Or you'll make the headlines again, as the youngest horse-thief in Britain.'

My day goes from bad to worse.

Mr Wolfe springs a spot-test on us in history, and I barely scrape through. In art I spend an hour making a carefully coiled clay pot and then drop it on the floor,

❀❀❀❀❀❀❀❀❀❀❀❀❀❀❀❀❀❀❀❀❀

squashing it flat; and in science I can't concentrate at all and almost set Sarah's hair on fire with a Bunsen burner. Sarah screams and Lawrie rolls his eyes at me across the lab and I end up with a punishment exercise to write out the legend *I must learn to respect laboratory equipment* one hundred times. Great.

'What about respecting my hair?' Sarah wants to know, but to be honest she has frazzled it more herself with excessive use of straighteners, so one small singed bit is not going to matter. Much.

I think the stresses of being the youngest horse-thief in Britain are beginning to tell.

After the bell, Lawrie corners me by the lockers.

'What's up with you?' he demands. 'You've been jumpy all day. Something wrong?'

'This is wrong,' I say, showing him the newspaper. 'We're in big trouble.'

'Don't panic,' Lawrie says, scanning the *Gazette*. 'Seddon was always likely to go to the press, always going to lie. We have to stay calm. It doesn't change anything.'

I bite my lip. 'I know. I do – it's just hard not to worry.'

Lawrie frowns. 'Tell me about it,' he says. 'I heard some

❀❀❀❀❀❀❀❀❀❀❀❀❀❀❀❀❀❀❀❀❀❀❀

bad news myself today. Seddon's bought two more horses. They're not in foal and they don't need breaking, but . . .'

My heart sinks. It feels like the final straw.

'Can we rescue them?' I ask. 'Get them out of there?'

'Don't even think about it, Coco,' he tells me. 'We may have got away with one rescue – so far – but trying another would be madness. The police think it's opportunist horse thieves at the moment – target the same place again and it's going to look very different. We can't risk it – it would put Caramel and Spirit in danger, blow the whole thing!'

'I hate him,' I huff, kicking at the wall in frustration. 'I really, really hate him.'

'You and me both,' Lawrie says. 'Look, we'll talk about this later . . .'

Sarah appears at my side and Lawrie gives her a dark look before striding away.

'What did *he* want?' she whispers.

'Just making some snarky comment about me burning the school down if I don't pay more attention,' I lie. 'He's such a charmer.'

'He fancies you,' Sarah says. 'I've seen the way he looks at you. All dark and smouldering.'

❀❀❀❀❀❀❀❀❀❀❀❀❀❀❀❀❀❀❀❀❀❀❀❀

'That's the way he looks at everyone,' I tell her.

'Maybe,' Sarah says, watching Lawrie disappear into the scrum of kids heading for the school gate. 'Maybe not. He likes you. Mark my words.'

I worry about that all the way home.

22

Back at Tanglewood, the little chocolate factory is silent and for the first time in almost a fortnight there is no aroma of melted chocolate drifting on the air. I head for the kitchen to make a flask of hot chocolate to take up to the cottage as usual, but the moment I step inside I can see that something is very wrong. Mum and Paddy are sitting at the big pine table, their faces grim.

'Everything OK?' I ask. 'Things going to plan with the order?'

'Factory's running like clockwork,' Paddy says. 'Thank goodness. We should have everything shipped off by the end of next week, but I've had to let the workers go early today, obviously . . .'

'I've been a fool,' Mum states flatly. 'I've been kidding

myself – so wrapped up in the business that I didn't notice what was going on right under my nose!'

'What was going on?' I ask warily.

Is this to do with the newspaper article? Have the police been round asking questions? Have Mum and Paddy worked out that I am not seeing my friends every after-noon, but wandering around the moors in the dark with a boy I barely know and a couple of stolen ponies?

I really hope not.

It's not even as though our rescue has changed anything – Seddon has just bought more ponies who will suffer in exactly the same way as Spirit and Caramel. There is no way to stop him, and the knowledge makes me feel crushed, hopeless.

Mum looks tired, with shadows under her eyes, smudged eyeliner and a hopeless, defeated tilt to her shoulders. Fear curls in my belly.

'Mum? What is it?'

She picks up a letter typed on the school's headed paper, her hand shaking. 'Oh, Coco . . . I was so proud of her, so sure she'd turned the corner. And now this!'

The penny drops.

✿✿✿✿✿✿✿✿✿✿✿✿✿✿✿✿✿✿✿✿✿

'Honey,' I say flatly, and Paddy nods.

'We've been asked to come into school to discuss her continued absences and erratic grades,' Mum says. 'But her report was excellent – how can things have gone downhill so fast? It doesn't make sense!'

'Let me ring the school and find out,' Paddy suggests.

'Not yet – we have to give Honey a chance to explain,' Mum argues. 'Perhaps it's a mix-up . . . there could be a perfectly reasonable explanation for it all.'

'Charlotte, if we just speak to Mr Keating . . .'

'No,' Mum pleads. 'We'll talk to Honey first. If something's been going on, I want to hear it from her. I'm her mother, she'll tell me the truth!'

I doubt that somehow, but I stay silent and put the kettle on. Instead of making a flask of hot chocolate I brew a pot of tea and raid the cupboard for Jammie Dodgers.

Family trouble, I text Lawrie quickly. Mum upset. Might be a bit late getting to the meeting place.

Will go without you, he texts back. Family comes first. Take care xx

I stare at the message, wide-eyed. Two kisses? Does

that mean anything, and if so, what? I would never have imagined that Lawrie was the kind of boy to add text kisses – after all, he can barely dredge up a smile for me most days.

By the time I've poured the tea and arranged the biscuits on a plate, Skye, Summer, Cherry and Honey come clattering in. Their chat fades to silence fast as they see Mum's face, tight-lipped.

'So . . . Honey?' she grates out, handing over the letter. 'Tell me this isn't true!'

Skye, Summer and Cherry huddle beside me, out of the line of fire, and Fred the dog nudges my hand with his nose. I stroke his ears and he leans against me, whining softly.

'It's a mistake, obviously,' Honey says, scanning the letter dismissively. 'Ridiculous. You've seen my report!'

'They can't both be right,' Mum says. 'What's going on, Honey?'

'Nothing! The computers at school must have been playing up, that's all – loads of things have been going wrong these last few days. Or maybe some stupid

❀❀❀❀❀❀❀❀❀❀❀❀❀❀❀❀❀❀❀❀❀

secretary has picked up last year's file? I am doing fine this term, you know I am!'

'We thought you were,' Paddy sighs. 'Now we're not too sure.'

Honey flings him an angry glance. 'Look, it's fine, all right?' she says. 'I was on the bus to school this morning – ask the others. And I was on the bus home; you can't argue with that. I haven't missed a day all term. Right, Summer? Skye? Cherry? We may not be in the same year but you must see me in the corridors sometimes . . .'

Cherry shrugs, and her eyes slide away from Honey's, evasive. She does not want to answer, and nobody can blame her – Honey has made her life a misery from day one.

Beside me, I can feel Summer shrink into herself, hiding behind her hair, arms wrapped around her body as if for protection. She was always the sister who stuck up for Honey, even when the rest of us despaired of her, but I'm not sure she will defend her now.

'I don't know,' she says in a whisper. 'I'm not at school all of the time any more, Honey, I have the day clinic thing twice a week. I . . . I can't say . . .'

❀❀❀❀❀❀❀❀❀❀❀❀❀❀❀❀❀❀❀❀❀❀❀❀

'I've seen you,' Skye chips in, taking the pressure off her twin. 'Once or twice. Maybe. Not for quite a while, though . . .'

'Oh, for goodness' sake!' Honey growls.

My sisters have never looked more uncomfortable. Nobody wants to break the 'sisters-don't-tell' rule, but all of us know it's time to stop covering up for Honey. I am glad I'm not at the high school, that nobody asks me. I would not want to tell how I see Honey come and go at all hours of the day and night, getting lifts from boys whose cars blare loud music and laughter. I would have to mention how she has been hanging out at the fair with hard-faced girls and tattooed boys, working on an art project that may or may not exist.

It's not even as if any of this seems to make my big sister happy.

'I don't know why they're saying all this,' she argues, shooting the twins a furious look. 'I'm in school every day, I told you. The letter's a mistake.'

'Well,' Paddy says, 'that's a relief. But we'll ring the school anyway, or call in to see Mr Keating tomorrow morning, let him know we got the letter. We can't ignore

❀❀❀❀❀❀❀❀❀❀❀❀❀❀❀❀❀❀❀❀❀❀❀❀❀

it, Honey. If it's some kind of computer error, they'll tell us – no harm done.'

'It's for the best,' Mum agrees. 'Set the record straight, sort it out.'

I watch Honey's face crumble, the confident mask replaced with anger, panic. Suddenly her excuses seem flimsy, desperate.

'I knew you wouldn't believe me!' she yells. 'You never do, any of you! Don't try and pretend that you care what I get up to – you really, really don't. All you care about are your horrible chocolates and that stupid order. Don't kid yourself – you're not going to make your fortunes. Those truffles will probably *poison* someone and then you'll be sorry! Sheesh, this whole family sucks!'

She storms out of the kitchen, slamming the door behind her.

'I don't know what to do,' Mum whispers. 'How did I miss this? How did I get it so wrong? Honey needs more help and support than I can give her – she's just so angry, so lost. No matter what I try to do, nothing ever changes.'

'We'll see Mr Keating in the morning, get to the bottom

✿✿✿✿✿✿✿✿✿✿✿✿✿✿✿✿✿✿✿✿✿✿✿✿

of it,' Paddy promises. 'We can't let her throw her life away like this.'

Honey's timing could not be worse – my family is stressed and struggling as it is; we really do not need more of Honey's dramas. Later, subdued and slightly shaken, we are eating a makeshift supper of cheese and vegetable pie heated up from the freezer when she flounces back into the kitchen.

'I've been speaking to Anthony,' she announces smugly, holding out her mobile. 'He's had exactly the same letter, and everyone knows he is the biggest swot in Somerset. He's probably never missed a school day in his life. So he reckons it is *definitely* a computer glitch because the school has just emailed him to apologize. So can you check your emails and see if we've had one too?'

'We're eating,' Paddy says patiently. 'I'll check in a minute.'

'This is my reputation at stake here,' Honey says. 'It's important!'

Mum stands up, tight-lipped, and fetches her laptop. She opens it, checks her mail, and there, sure enough, is an email from Exmoor High. '*A faulty software installation*

204

on the school IT system has resulted in some confusion, with warning letters being sent to students who are in fact performing very well at present,' she reads. 'How odd . . . I've never heard of anything like that before.'

'It happens all the time, apparently,' Honey says. 'So. A problem with the software system. OK? Don't all say sorry at once.'

'Well . . . I am sorry if we jumped to the wrong conclusion,' Mum says.

'Thank you,' Honey snaps. 'Now, I have a ton of homework, so I'd better get on with it.'

We watch her go.

'*If* we jumped to the wrong conclusion,' Mum repeats. 'But I don't think we did somehow. Take a look at this . . .'

She hands the laptop over to Paddy, who reads it carefully. 'It's from the school's email address all right. And the header looks official too . . .'

'Look closely,' Mum says.

We look at the address: *Exmoor High School, Graystone Lane* . . .

'What am I looking for?' Paddy frowns.

'They've spelt "Greystone" wrong,' Mum says. 'And I

really don't think the school would make that mistake, do you?'

Paddy raises an eyebrow. 'Ah,' he says. 'Not so good. The punctuation is a bit dodgy too. It's from the school's email, but . . .'

'Something odd is going on here,' Mum says, her mouth settling into a thin line. 'Let's see what Mr Keating has to say about it in the morning.'

23

On Friday afternoon, after school, I am in the music room auditioning for Miss Noble; next door in the hall, the orchestra kids are warming up in a screech of trumpet blasts and cello twangs and bursts of unruly saxophone. Soon, with luck, I will be joining them.

I am playing a violin piece I have composed myself, and Miss Noble is looking quite amazed and very impressed. I think. I hit a few dud notes because playing violin in a classroom is very different from playing violin in an oak tree, but I think this just adds to the atmosphere. After all, I am twelve years old and mostly self-taught. Miss Noble will not be expecting perfection.

I don't think I will miss riding lessons at all, not once I am playing violin solos in the orchestra.

❀❀❀❀❀❀❀❀❀❀❀❀❀❀❀❀❀❀❀❀❀❀❀

The teacher holds her hand up, smiling. 'Thank you, Coco,' she says. 'A very . . . unusual style of playing. Full of character.'

I grin.

'Sadly, I won't be able to offer you a place in the orchestra on this occasion,' she tells me, and my face falls. 'You have a certain raw talent, but I'm afraid there's a little way to go before you reach orchestra standard. You would need to be able to read music too. Some lessons might be a good idea.'

'It's a no?' I double-check, feeling as crestfallen as if I've just been voted off *The X Factor*. 'Are you sure? If I could just play it again, with my gloves on, because that's how I usually do it . . .'

'Not this time, Coco,' Miss Noble says kindly. 'Take some lessons and try out again at the high school.'

I put my violin away in its case, pull on my panda hat and grab my schoolbag. The world is full of disappointments. Music teachers who do not recognize genius when they see it, landowners who treat their ponies like dirt, sisters who break the rules, boys who sulk and growl and sign off their texts with kisses just to confuse you. Lawrie

❀ ❀

Marshall actually came up to me today in the lunch queue and asked how things were at home, and I just gulped and said everything was fine because I really did not want any kind of fuss with Sarah and the others around. They noticed anyhow and teased me all day about Lawrie fancying me, which did not help my stress levels, seriously.

There's an icy bite in the air as I trudge out towards the school gate. My heart is heavier than my schoolbag until I spot three familiar figures sitting on the wall.

'Coco!' Cherry calls, jumping down and running across the playground. 'Over here! We've come to kidnap you!'

'We're taking you for tea,' Skye adds, hooking an arm through mine. 'We went to the riding stables and some boy with smouldering eyes told us you'd given up on lessons, and that you'd be here, pursuing your musical career . . .'

'Lawrie Marshall,' Cherry says, with a knowing look. 'He is *so* not the way you described him.'

'He looks quite cool,' Summer tells me.

'Hot, you mean,' Skye corrects her twin. 'Anyway, here we are. Have you got your stuff? Shall we go?'

I allow myself to be led out of school and down towards

the seafront cafe, my sisters talking all the time. It feels good to be with them and takes some of the sting out of being turned down for the orchestra. I remind myself that many great artists and musicians were not appreciated properly in their lifetimes.

'So why have you kidnapped me?' I ask, as we tumble into the warm, brightly lit cafe. 'Not that I am complaining, obviously . . .'

'Ah. World War Three is raging at home,' Skye explains as we order three big hot chocolates with whipped cream and chocolate flakes and a modest skinny latte for Summer. 'You do *not* want to be there right now. Honey's in *so* much trouble – Mum is furious and Paddy is banging the table with his fist and they are all waiting for Dad to call from Australia . . .'

We slide into a window seat, the sea in the distance grey and ominous in the dusk, and for once my sisters' faces are serious.

'So . . . what happened?' I ask.

'She's been expelled from school,' Summer whispers. 'Excluded, thrown out, asked to leave . . . and Anthony too!'

✿✿✿✿✿✿✿✿✿✿✿✿✿✿✿✿✿✿✿✿✿✿✿

I blink. 'But . . . why? Skipping lessons?'

'Worse than that,' Skye tells me. 'Mum and Paddy went in to see Mr Keating this morning, and everything came out. Honey's been truanting for months, going into Minehead on the school bus and then disappearing off to town. Turns out she'd met this boy who works at the fairground, and she was hanging out with him and his friends . . .'

That pulls me up short.

'I saw her,' I whisper. 'After the firework display in town – she was with these scary-looking girls, talking to a boy with tattoos. She told me she was working on an art project. I believed her. I am so stupid . . .'

'We've all been stupid,' Skye says. 'Trying to cover up for her, hoping she'd wise up and sort herself out. It's been going on way too long.'

'She's been fobbing the teachers off with forged letters saying she was ill,' Cherry tells me. 'Really ill – the letters talked about blood tests and scans and stays in hospital. She didn't say what was wrong, exactly, but she implied it was serious. The teachers were really upset, and nobody wanted to say anything.'

❀❀❀❀❀❀❀❀❀❀❀❀❀❀❀❀❀❀❀❀❀❀

'Think they reckoned our family had enough troubles right now,' Summer says quietly. 'With me having . . . an eating disorder and everything. That's why they've been asking how she was, passing on worksheets and homework. Anthony was the main go-between, passing on letters and collecting work. I guess that means he's been doing most of it for her too.'

I bite my lip. 'But . . . how come Honey's school report didn't say anything?' I ask. 'It said she had perfect attendance, and that her grades were fine. And . . . what's Anthony got to do with all this, anyway?'

Cherry sips her hot chocolate. 'Mum and Paddy were there most of the day,' she says. 'It was a major investigation – Anthony's parents had to come in too, and everyone was trying to find out what was happening.'

'Honey's had Anthony dangling on a string for ages now,' Summer goes on. 'She's been going down to see him once or twice a week, in between seeing her fairground friends. Anthony has a crush on her; he'd do pretty much anything to please her.'

'And he's really brainy,' Cherry reminds me. 'Some kind of computer genius.'

❀❀❀❀❀❀❀❀❀❀❀❀❀❀❀❀❀❀❀❀❀❀❀❀❀

'So . . . ?'

Skye dunks her chocolate flake and bites into the end. 'You won't believe it,' she says. 'He's been hacking into the school computer system. He altered Honey's report and made it look like she'd got good grades and perfect attendance, and he tweaked some of her coursework marks too . . . scary!'

I almost choke on my hot chocolate, ending up with a dollop of whipped cream on my nose. It's not a good look.

'No way,' I breathe. 'That's . . . major! No wonder they've kicked her out, and Anthony. She must have known she couldn't get away with it!'

'I don't think she cared either way,' Skye shrugs. 'And Anthony's clever, he had it all planned out. He was sending letters to the school, as well, supposedly from the hospital, and from Mum and Paddy. Nightmare.'

'Last night's email blew it all,' Cherry explains. 'If Anthony had got the school address right, they might never have been found out.'

My head is spinning. Expelled from school? I don't think even Honey can wriggle out of this one. Finally, after years

❀❀❀❀❀❀❀❀❀❀❀❀❀❀❀❀❀❀❀❀❀❀

of pushing the boundaries, breaking the rules and behaving badly, my big sister has reached the end of the line. It's terrifying but kind of a relief at the same time.

'I should have lied,' Summer says into the silence. 'Last night. Said I saw Honey around at school, so Mum believed her excuses . . .'

'No,' Skye cuts in. 'You shouldn't, Summer. And nor should I. We didn't drop her in it, we were just honest. It's time we dumped that old "sisters-don't-tell" rule because Honey needs help, you know that – we've all known it for a while. She wasn't always this way . . .'

I frown, trying to remember the way things were before Dad left. It all seems hazy and long ago, a perfect world where the sun always shone and nothing ever went wrong, but I'm pretty sure it wasn't like that really. I do remember Honey, bright and beautiful and kind and confident, always laughing, always Dad's favourite.

Then he left us, and Honey turned from golden girl to rebel just about overnight. She yelled and shouted and blamed Mum for letting him go, but Mum couldn't have stopped him, of course – none of us could.

'What happens now?' I ask.

❀❀❀❀❀❀❀❀❀❀❀❀❀❀❀❀❀❀❀❀❀❀

'Paddy took us home, told us everything,' Skye shrugs. 'Mum's gutted. She called Dad in Sydney but he's in a meeting, so they're waiting for him to ring back, and Honey just looks sort of shell-shocked. You could cut the atmosphere with a knife. Paddy said it might be an idea to go and stay with friends tonight, stay out of the firing line. So Mum rang Tia's mum and she says we can all come over for an epic sleepover, me and Summer and Cherry and you. And Millie from school, and Cherry's friend Haruna.'

'We grabbed our PJs and sleeping bags, and your stuff too,' Cherry adds. 'Paddy dropped us at the riding stable to collect you, and when you weren't there we asked that stable boy and walked up to the school.'

I blink. 'So I have to go to Tia's?'

'Well, that's what Mum arranged,' Summer says. 'We should all stick together because I really don't recommend going back to Tanglewood right now.'

I try to picture the sleepover, a crush of teenage girls wrapped in duvets and sleeping bags, eating pizza and popcorn and dissecting every last detail of Honey's fall from grace. I don't think I could stomach it.

❀❀❀❀❀❀❀❀❀❀❀❀❀❀❀❀❀❀❀❀❀❀❀❀❀

'Couldn't I go to Sarah's house instead?' I ask. 'I don't think I can face a big gang of your mates right now . . . it's quite a lot to take in.'

Skye frowns. 'Well, I suppose it'd be OK,' she says. 'As long as we know where you are. If you can just check with Sarah . . .'

I tap out a quick message on my mobile and a few moments later a reply bleeps through. No problem. See you soon

'It's fine,' I say. 'I can stay as long as I want.'

'Great.' Summer looks at her watch. 'I'll text Mum and let her know. We should go, y'know, we don't want to miss the six o'clock bus. The girls will be waiting.'

'We'll walk you along to Sarah's,' Skye says, ushering me out into the street. 'Make sure you get there OK.'

I know better than to argue – my sisters are in protective mode and it's not hard to work out why, what with everything that's happening at home. Skye and Summer would freak if they knew what I'd been up to these past few weeks – they still think I am six years old, some cute little kid in patched dungarees with a pet spider in a matchbox.

They deliver me to Sarah's gate, watch me walk along

the path and ring the bell, then sprint along to the bus stop as the Kitnor bus heaves into view, waving as they pile on board.

'See you tomorrow!' Skye yells. 'Have fun!'

The door opens and Sarah peers out. 'Oh,' she says. 'Hi, Coco. Didn't expect to see you tonight.'

'Flying visit,' I tell her. 'I've just come from orchestra practice, and I wanted to check whether we had maths homework this weekend or not.'

'We do,' Sarah says, frowning. 'Fractions and decimals for that test on Monday.'

'OK,' I say brightly. 'Great. See you then!'

I check that the bus has vanished, then wave and walk back down the path. Sarah watches me, puzzled, as I walk towards the lone figure on the corner, a boy leaning moodily against the wall, eating chips, checking his mobile, his bike silhouetted in the lamplight.

24

We finish up the chips and ride out of town, along the quiet lanes towards the hazel copse, me sitting on the bike seat with my arms round Lawrie's waist while he stands up, pedalling hard. I am still in school uniform, my schoolbag slung across my body, my violin case tied on to the back of the bike with bungees. The wind lifts my hair but it doesn't quite blow away my troubles – not today.

'What's up?' Lawrie asks finally, as we ditch the bike and hike up through the heather towards the ruined cottage. 'Why the mystery text? Friday's normally my day because of working at the stables.'

'And Saturday and Sunday are supposed to be mine, but you came up anyhow,' I remind him. 'I'm just fed up. I failed my audition for the school orchestra.'

❀❀❀❀❀❀❀❀❀❀❀❀❀❀❀❀❀❀❀❀❀❀❀

'Well, you can't be good at everything,' he shrugs.

I want to ask why not, or point out that I am not asking to be good at everything, just one thing, for now at least, but it seems pointless.

'You can play for me, anyway,' Lawrie is saying. 'I don't know much about music but I quite like the sound of the violin. Sort of sad, but I bet I'd like it. Will you?'

'I might,' I tell him. 'Sometime. Maybe.'

'Is something else wrong?'

I sigh. 'My family are in crisis – again. Don't want to go home, don't want to talk about it . . .'

'Fair enough,' he shrugs.

The evening is bitterly cold and the dark velvet sky is sprinkled with a million stars. It's beautiful but freezing, the kind of night when your breath hovers in little clouds just beyond your lips. We trudge on in silence, but I can't keep quiet. The day's disasters are playing over and over in my head like a newsreel.

'My big sister's been expelled,' I blurt suddenly. 'She is fifteen years old, seeing a boy from the fairground, truanting from school. She got her friend to hack into the school computer system to fake school reports and told the teachers she had a serious illness. They're waiting for my dad to ring from Australia to decide what to do, but whatever it is won't be good. Honey has been pushing her luck for way too long.'

I pause for breath. For someone who doesn't want to talk about it, I am doing OK. I tell Lawrie about Honey's part in the stable fire this summer, her attempt to run away; how only a few weeks ago at the start of the autumn term, she was reported missing and turned up next day, completely oblivious to the panic she'd caused. The police warned her then they would call social services if she got into trouble again.

This is a different kind of trouble, but just as serious; is that why Paddy wanted us out of the house tonight? Are social services at Tanglewood right now, making notes, shaking their heads, planning my sister's future? I feel sick just thinking about it.

'OK. Not good,' Lawrie is saying. 'No wonder you don't want to go home – it sounds a bit full-on.'

'It is,' I say into the darkness, and suddenly an avalanche of hurt spills out, defensive, despairing.

'Everyone thinks we're so perfect, but we're really not.

✿✿✿✿✿✿✿✿✿✿✿✿✿✿✿✿✿✿✿✿✿✿✿

We live in a big house, but it doesn't belong to us – it's Grandma Kate's, and since Dad left we've had to run it as a B&B to make ends meet. We need the chocolate business to take off and we have this big order just now, but Paddy's had to halt production to sort this mess out. Oh yeah, and one of my sisters is anorexic and one is trying to smash what's left of our family into little bits . . .'

'I'm sorry, Coco,' Lawrie says.

I tilt my chin up proudly as we approach the ruined cottage. 'I don't usually go around telling other people my troubles. Don't want anyone feeling sorry for me.'

Lawrie nods. 'I understand. I won't tell anyone.'

'You'd better not.'

A thin whinnying sound drifts down through the darkness, and I stop short, frowning.

'The ponies,' Lawrie says, running forward through the heather. 'Quick . . . something's wrong!'

We push through the gate to Jasmine Cottage to find Spirit trotting jerkily through the overgrown garden, kicking at her swollen stomach, pushing herself against the hedge, crying out while Caramel paces patiently alongside her.

'She's foaling,' Lawrie says, his face grave. 'I knew she was close, but I thought we had a little more time . . .'

Guilt and panic curdle inside me, cold and sour. I checked the Internet for information on delivering a foal, but with all the chaos at Tanglewood lately, I failed to follow it up. I made time to bake cupcakes and design posters, but not to find out how best to help a pony who needed me.

I can't remember a thing from the online article. What kind of a would-be vet am I? 'What do we do?' I ask.

'Get lanterns and hay and hope for the best,' Lawrie says.

He takes Spirit's head collar and presses his face against hers, whispering softly, quietening, calming her, walking her up and down while I light the lanterns and spread hay across the floor of the ruined kitchen. After a while, he leads Spirit in.

'Her waters have broken,' he tells me. 'It shouldn't take too long now – if things are straightforward she won't need us at all. Let's just hope that they are . . .'

Caramel crowds into the cottage kitchen, uneasy, curious, and Spirit stumbles to her knees on the hay, nostrils flaring. Lawrie soothes her and she slumps on to her side, tail swishing, eyes wide.

'There must be something I can do?' I ask. On TV, when babies are being born in unexpected places, people boil kettles and tear up clean sheets and gather towels while they wait for the ambulance to arrive. I am not sure it is the same for ponies, but even if it were, there is no way here to get hot water or clean linen, and no ambulance will be arriving any time soon.

'Well,' Lawrie says, 'how about you play that violin for us?'

'What, now?'

Lawrie nods, and although the whole idea of it is obviously crazy, I reach for my violin case, lifting out the glossy, curvy violin. Every time I play, my heart lifts up with music and takes me far away, to a place where anything is possible. Even when Mum banned me from playing in the house, even when my sisters made jokes about screeching ghosts and cats being strangled, nothing could spoil it for me . . . until today's failed audition. Gloom floods me all over again, but I push it away, determined. If anything can calm the crackle of tension and fear in the air, the violin can.

❀ ❀

Spirit groans softly in the lamplight, dark eyes fringed with long lashes fixed on me as I start to play. Music swirls around the shadowy corners, filling up the darkness with a haunting lament that slowly builds into something brighter, braver. I play for ages, until Spirit's breathing steadies, until Lawrie grins in the lamplight.

'I think she's almost there,' he says. 'Look!'

I put my bow down, kneeling beside Lawrie as the foal is born, long legs first, wrapped in a sticky membrane. Time seems to slow. As I hold my breath, the head appears, and then finally the foal slides out into the hay and I am wiping the sticky membrane from its face as if I have done it a million times before. Lawrie is grinning and Spirit is resting now, nudging the foal gently.

'He's perfect,' I say, and my eyes brim with happy tears because in spite of everything that is messed up and wrong with my world, the newborn foal really is perfect, a kind of miracle.

'We could call him Star,' Lawrie suggests. 'It's such a clear sky tonight you can see whole constellations . . .'

'Perfect,' I say again.

My memory dredges up what I read on the Internet,

❀❀❀❀❀❀❀❀❀❀❀❀❀❀❀❀❀❀❀❀❀❀❀

and I know that we have to let Spirit and her foal rest now before she breaks the cord. The website said something about iodine to disinfect, but we don't have any and I try not to worry; there wouldn't have been any in the wild, after all.

'It'll be a couple of hours before she delivers the placenta,' Lawrie says. 'I'll stay, obviously.'

'Me too,' I whisper. 'I can't go back to the house tonight; I told you.'

Then Lawrie makes a tiny fire in the grate so we don't all die of frostbite, and Spirit struggles to her feet and the cord breaks, and there doesn't seem to be any need for iodine.

'The violin was good,' he says. 'Who needs the school orchestra? You are clearly more of a ruined-cottage violinist, gloves and icicles and jasmine in the hair, at one with nature.'

I laugh. 'You're a music expert now? Well, whatever, I'll take the compliment. My fan club consists of you and two ponies.'

Lawrie grins. 'Three, actually. Star is your biggest fan. And we all have very good taste.'

I stroke the foal so gently that it feels like I am holding

✿✿✿✿✿✿✿✿✿✿✿✿✿✿✿✿✿✿✿✿✿✿✿✿✿

my breath. Spirit looks on, calm and trusting. She's wrong to trust me, though. If anything had gone wrong tonight, the ponies would have been in danger – because of me.

I thought I had things all mapped out with no margin for error – but my plans are unravelling by the minute. Life is not a box of chocolates, a pick 'n' mix where I can choose just what I want; it turns out that someone has tricked me, switched the whole box for something less appealing. Lately, more and more, I find myself biting into something tough, tasteless, stale; something that leaves a bad taste in my mouth.

It turns out I am hopeless at the violin, and how am I supposed to stop bullies like Seddon and save the world when my own family is falling to bits right before my eyes? I am keeping so many secrets, telling so many lies to so many people that I can barely sleep at night. Not even Cherry, Sarah, Amy and Jayde know the whole story – they just know snippets of what's happening, my own edited version.

My big sister isn't the only one breaking the rules, the law.

Caramel comes close, nuzzling my hair, and I feel the

❀❀❀❀❀❀❀❀❀❀❀❀❀❀❀❀❀❀❀❀❀❀❀❀

gentle pressure of a hand on my shoulder. 'Hey,' Lawrie says. 'Don't go all slushy on me now . . .'

I wipe a sleeve across my eyes, fierce, furious. 'I'm not,' I lie. 'I just . . . got something in my eye. A speck of dust or something . . . OK?'

Lawrie nods, and I reflect that there is something to be said for having a mate like him, someone who just gets on with stuff and doesn't try to dig out your deepest, darkest secrets. And it is difficult to be sad for too long when a scruffy Exmoor pony is breathing down your neck and chewing the hood of your duffel coat, seriously.

I huddle next to the fire beside Lawrie, who hands me apples and chocolate, and we watch as Star battles to his feet, long legs buckling and sliding as he nudges against Spirit and begins to feed. My fingers begin to thaw a little as I hold them out to the flames.

'What will happen about your sister?' Lawrie asks quietly. 'What will your family do?'

'I don't know,' I admit. 'Mum and Paddy have given her so many chances . . . but the truth is, she doesn't want to be here, doesn't want to be a part of our family. That hurts – for all of us. She used to be Dad's favourite;

she thinks that if he were still around things would be different. Thing is, Dad's moved on – he never bothered seeing us when he was in London, and now he lives on the other side of the world.'

'We're not so different, you and me,' Lawrie muses. 'Our dads both let us down. What's your stepdad like?'

'Great,' I say easily. 'Paddy's good fun and he makes Mum happy – that's the biggest thing. He's working really hard to make us into a family, and I think he does care about Honey – if she'd just give him a chance!'

'Sounds like one of the good guys,' Lawrie says. 'You're lucky. Not everyone is like that.'

I shrug. 'Well, most people are OK, I guess . . .'

'Huh,' he says. 'I used to think that too, once. After Dad left, Mum wanted a new start, to put some distance between us and him. She got a job as a housekeeper for some holiday cottages; the work was easy and there was a rent-free flat thrown in. Then it all went pear-shaped, and now we're stuck here, trapped.'

'Trapped?' I echo. 'How come?'

Lawrie shrugs. The shutters come down again as if he has changed his mind, said too much.

✿✿✿✿✿✿✿✿✿✿✿✿✿✿✿✿✿✿✿✿✿✿✿✿✿

'I'll tell you sometime,' he says, getting up to fetch more firewood. 'Maybe. Don't worry about it. What does it matter how messed up our lives are right now? It won't be forever. One day soon you'll be a violin-playing vet, travelling from place to place on horseback, handing out panda cupcakes to the poor and needy . . . and I'll run my own stables back home in Cumbria. We'll look back at all this and laugh.'

'You think?' I ask.

'No, probably not,' he says. 'Maybe we'll end our days in prison. Coco and Marshall, the notorious under-age Exmoor horse rustlers . . .' He pulls his woolly scarf up over his nose, gangster style, raising his hands in surrender, and the two of us dissolve into laughter.

A couple of hours later, the birthing is safely over and Lawrie has cleared everything away and brought in fresh hay for Spirit and Star and Caramel. We sit for hours, huddled in blankets beside the crackling fire, watching the three ponies and talking about an imaginary future where no animals are ever ill-treated.

'Panda hats will be considered the height of fashion,' Lawrie declares. 'And all music lessons will be conducted a minimum of ten feet off the ground, in the branches of an oak tree.'

'All animals will be equal,' I add. 'Cruelty will be abolished and annoying Year Six boys with cake addictions and bullying tendencies will be hoisted up the school flagpole.'

'Certificates of excellence will be awarded for science students who succeed in singeing their own hair with a Bunsen burner. I don't know why we don't go into politics. We'd soon get this country straightened out – we'd be unstoppable!'

My laughter fades and I remember that in real life we don't have quite so much to laugh about, but I have never been the kind of person to accept defeat.

I bite my lip. 'Listen, Lawrie,' I say. 'I know it's risky, but . . . we have to rescue Seddon's new ponies. We don't have a choice, you know that, don't you?'

'Coco, just hold on –'

'We can't leave them there!' I argue. 'Seddon's a thug, you know that – he won't treat them well. We don't have to bring them up here – that would endanger Caramel and Spirit and Star. But if we get them out and take

❀❀❀❀❀❀❀❀❀❀❀❀❀❀❀❀❀❀❀❀❀❀❀❀

them somewhere safe – like the riding school perhaps – well, that would be a message to the police that we're not stealing them for profit. We could send a note to the police and to the *Gazette*, maybe, about how Seddon treats his animals . . .'

Lawrie frowns. 'It could work. We could tip off the police and the papers, then Jean and Roy wouldn't get into trouble. Maybe someone will actually check up on Seddon and find out what he's like. It wouldn't be stealing . . . more moving the ponies around. I think you're on to something, Coco!'

'I know I am,' I tell him. 'So . . . tomorrow night? I'll draft some letters for the police and the newspaper.'

'Meet in the woods by Blue Downs House then?' Lawrie suggests. 'At midnight?'

'I'll be there. And . . . I'll never forget this night, Lawrie. Spirit and Star . . . and, well, everything.'

'Nor me.'

I yawn and stretch, suddenly aware of how late it must be. Lawrie puts together a nest of cushions and blankets and I curl inside it, bone-weary, while he banks up the fire with fresh logs.

❀❀❀❀❀❀❀❀❀❀❀❀❀❀❀❀❀❀❀❀❀❀❀

I wake achey and cold, with the heavy arm of the school's moodiest boy flung over me beneath the blankets that cocoon us both, his breath warm on my neck, his hand holding mine.

Departures

25

The fallout from Honey's expulsion from school is still settling when I return home on Saturday morning. The chocolate factory is deserted, the kitchen looks like a bomb has hit it and Mum and Paddy look shattered, as if they haven't slept at all. Well, maybe they haven't.

Honey is stretched out on one of the blue velvet sofas, watching our *Bambi* DVD and eating crumpets. She looks unbothered, as if today is just any old Saturday and not the day after she got kicked out of Exmoor High. I remember the time I first watched *Bambi*, years ago when I was little, with Honey, Summer and Skye. I was mad about animals even then and I loved it – right up until the moment that Bambi's mum got shot. I cried so hard then that Mum had to switch it off, and my sisters

✿✿✿✿✿✿✿✿✿✿✿✿✿✿✿✿✿✿✿✿✿✿

grumbled and told me I was a baby, and not to be stupid because it was just a movie.

There's a lump in my throat as I flop down beside Honey now.

'You OK?' I ask. 'Are you grounded again?'

'Don't think so,' she shrugs. 'What's the point? They know I'll find a way round it. Besides, I don't care any more. I'm out of here!'

My mind buzzes with past threats of boarding school. 'What d'you mean?'

'Ask Mum,' Honey says. 'She and Paddy have got what they wanted – to be rid of me.'

'That's not true!' I argue. 'You're twisting things round!'

She shrugs. 'Whatever. It doesn't matter because I got what I wanted too. Sorry to ditch you, little sis, but I finally get to escape this dump. Apparently boarding school is too expensive – trust Paddy, stingy with the cash right to the last – but hey, this time it works in my favour. I'm going out to Australia to live with Dad. This time next week I'll be on a flight to Sydney!'

I feel cold all over. My big sister is a chancer, a drama

✿✿✿✿✿✿✿✿✿✿✿✿✿✿✿✿✿✿✿✿✿✿✿✿✿✿

queen, a rule-breaker. She's lazy, rebellious and sometimes downright bitchy, but I love her to pieces and I cannot imagine life without her.

'You can't!' I whisper. 'What about us?'

'What about you?' Honey asks. 'You've made your choice, Coco. You just can't see how Paddy has ruined this family, can you? If it wasn't for him, Dad and Mum might have been back together by now.'

'Honey, you know that's not true!'

'Well, it was possible, wasn't it?' she snaps. 'Until Mum married that loser! Now she puts him first the whole time. Admit it, we have hardly seen them this last week or two!'

'That's because of the department store order,' I argue. 'You're not being fair. Mum has done everything in her power to help you and Paddy is trying his very best too!'

Honey shrugs. 'His best isn't good enough,' she says. 'Not for me. Paddy doesn't belong here – he's not my dad, and he never will be!'

She picks up a fluffy cushion and hugs it to her, her lower lip quivering. I think Honey is a whole lot more bothered by all this than she is letting on. 'I can't get

❀❀❀❀❀❀❀❀❀❀❀❀❀❀❀❀❀❀❀❀❀❀

along with Cherry either – and the rest of you are so totally taken in by her,' she goes on. 'She's pushed me out – with Mum, with Shay, even with you . . .'

'No way!' I protest. 'Nobody could ever do that! Honey, please don't go away. If you could only try harder at school, stay away from the fairground crowd and just calm down . . . it's not too late!'

Honey shakes her head. 'I think it is. I've tried too, Coco – really I have. I just can't seem to get anything right, and the whole school thing has gone way too far. They wouldn't have me back even if I wanted them to, and trust me, I don't. I made one massive mistake trusting Anthony. It was his idea, about hacking into the school system and changing my report – I should have known we'd never get away with it. And now he's not even speaking to me – he says it's all my fault!'

I remember seeing Anthony at one of our beach parties in the summer, a misfit loner whose puppy-dog eyes trailed after Honey wherever she went. He had a major crush on her, but of course, Anthony has never even been on my sister's radar. It's all too easy to imagine him thinking up plots and plans to hike up her school grades, to please her, hoping she might see him differently. Instead it all backfired, and Anthony's perfect school career is over in one dramatic fall from grace. I guess that would cure a crush, all right.

'The truth is I don't fit in here any more,' Honey is saying. 'I am a walking disaster area. My friends are the kind of kids who think it's cool to break the rules. As for boys, the ones I like have "trouble" stamped all over them. And when things go wrong, not one of them is anywhere to be seen.'

'So change your friends, pick nicer boyfriends,' I say. 'You can still turn things around. Start over!'

'I'm going to,' Honey says. 'In Australia. I'll miss you, Coco-pops, of course I will, but we can stay in touch on Skype and SpiderWeb. I have tried about a million fresh starts here, you know that – I need something different. Dad's stepped up to the mark, finally – he's going to find a good school, hire tutors, make sure I pass some exams. He does care, Coco!'

'Of course he does,' I say, although I have to admit there has never been much evidence of it before. I can't say that to Honey, though.

❀❀❀❀❀❀❀❀❀❀❀❀❀❀❀❀❀❀❀❀❀❀❀

'I still miss Dad,' she tells me. 'Every day. And the rest of you seem to have forgotten him, and it makes me feel like such a freak for even caring . . .'

'We all miss him,' I tell her, and because there really isn't any more to say I put my arms round my big sister and hold her tight. She hugs me back, her face pressed against my shoulder, her beautiful hair soft beneath my fingers.

I look up and see that the DVD has reached the part where Bambi's mother gets shot, but this time it's Honey who's crying.

I sit at one end of the blue sofa, writing letters to the newspaper and to the police about Seddon and the way he treats his ponies, while Honey huddles at the other end, curled up under the blanket made of crochet squares she has had since she was tiny.

My sisters come home at midday and Mum and Paddy call a family meeting in the kitchen. Everyone is there except Honey, who has fallen asleep in the living room, the tail end of *Bambi* playing softly in the background.

'Is it true that you're sending her away?' I blurt out, as soon as Mum sits down. 'You can't, Mum, it's cruel!'

✿✿✿✿✿✿✿✿✿✿✿✿✿✿✿✿✿✿✿✿✿✿✿

Skye kicks me hard under the table. 'Shut UP, Coco!' she whispers. 'That's not helping!'

Mum's eyes fill with tears, and I am instantly ashamed. 'It's not what I want,' she explains in a wobbly voice. 'It's what your sister wants . . . what she's wanted all along. She has used up all her chances here. She needs discipline, rules, support – we've tried to give her those things, Coco, you know that. It hasn't worked. Everyone is in agreement here, Mr Keating, the school counsellor, Honey's social worker . . .'

I gulp. 'She has a social worker?'

'Social services are trying to help us,' Paddy says. 'They've been aware of the problems since the summer, when Honey ran away. Once the police were involved, they were involved – but they want to help, Coco, we all do. We just want what's best for Honey.'

'And what's that?' Skye asks.

'A fresh start,' Paddy says. 'A chance to get away from the kids she's been seeing – well, most of them aren't kids, of course, and that's part of the problem. It's almost like a cry for help, and let's face it, the gentle approach hasn't worked. We need to do something different.'

'Boarding school was one option,' Mum says. 'We looked into it, and there were a couple of places that gave great support to troubled teens like Honey – but right now, we can't afford the fees. If we knew that this big chocolate order was going to be a success it might be different, but we can't predict what will happen.'

'So Honey's dad has stepped in,' Paddy says. 'He's found a day school in Sydney that promises good grades and one-to-one tuition and counselling for girls like Honey.'

'What does that mean?' Summer asks. 'Who are these "girls like Honey"? Is it some kind of Australian boot camp?'

'Not at all,' Mum promises. 'It's very strict but very fair, a private school with a good reputation academically. It has an exceptional ethos, though – one that could really help Honey. It's all about encouraging self-esteem and healing hurts, turning negatives into positives. We've spoken with the head teacher, and she seems confident they can turn your sister around.'

'But . . . why does it have to be on the other side of the world?' I plead.

❀❀❀❀❀❀❀❀❀❀❀❀❀❀❀❀❀❀❀❀❀❀❀

Mum sighs. 'Because we don't know of any schools here that offer this kind of help,' she says honestly. 'And if we did, we probably wouldn't be able to afford them. Luckily, this particular school is near to Greg, and the fees are affordable, just about, if both we and Greg chip in.'

'You're sending her away,' I whisper.

Mum's eyes fill with tears. 'Coco, it's just until the summer . . . we can review things then, see what Honey wants. And, Coco, she wants this – a fresh start, away from bad influences, in a school that promises to get her back on the right track. She wants to be with Greg, you know that. I don't want this any more than you do, but we have to do something, Coco your sister is right on the edge.'

I think of Dad, who is so busy with his high-flying business in Sydney that he barely has time to speak to us on Skype at Christmas; he has been known to forget our birthdays, our ages, our interests. OK, he is thousands of miles away in Australia, I know, but even when he lived in London he was kind of hopeless. I sometimes wonder if he'd forget he had kids at all unless Mum was there to remind him.

❀❀❀❀❀❀❀❀❀❀❀❀❀❀❀❀❀❀❀❀❀❀❀

I really hope the day school is good because if things are left to Dad, Honey won't be on the edge for much longer – she'll tumble right over it and go into freefall.

26

Lawrie whistles as I swerve my bike to a halt by the woodland at Blue Downs House just before midnight, stepping through the trees to greet me. 'Hey,' he says, looking at me so intently I can't quite meet his gaze. 'Everything OK at home?'

'Not really,' I tell him. 'Everything's about as bad as it possibly can be. I'll tell you later.'

'Where do your parents think you are right now?'

'Sarah's,' I say. 'Trust me, they have so much on their plate right now they won't even think of checking up.'

'Sure you want to do this?'

'Try and stop me,' I huff. 'I'm determined to get one thing right this week if it kills me . . .'

We walk slowly through the woods and past the

❀❀❀❀❀❀❀❀❀❀❀❀❀❀❀❀❀❀❀❀❀❀❀❀❀

paddock, up to the edge of the stable yard. We watch the farmhouse until the last lights are extinguished, then unhook the gate and creep softly round the perimeter of the yard.

The ponies are stabled separately, side by side at the end of the block. One is a chestnut, the other a roan, and both are stocky, steady, calm. I falter for a moment; maybe Seddon will treat these two properly? Then I remember the way he treated Caramel, the state Spirit was in, and I know we have no choice but to carry on. The new ponies may be OK right now, but it's just a matter of time before Seddon crushes their spirit too. Getting these two out will blow the whistle on what he is doing, trigger an investigation and maybe stop him from ever working with animals again.

As we lead them out across the yard a plaintive, whining bark rasps out across the silence. Lawrie swears under his breath. 'Sheesh . . . I forgot about the blinkin' dog!'

He hands me the reins of the chestnut pony and moves towards the skinny mongrel quickly, palm outstretched, whispering softly. The guard dog quietens almost at once, but

❖ ❖

not before I see the curve of its ribs in the moonlight, the hollow of its belly. The dog is thinner than ever, shivering, cowering, tied to an outdoor kennel with a short rope that keeps her bowl of water tantalizingly out of reach.

'Think anyone heard?' Lawrie asks, petting the dog's head, glancing up towards the house. 'I hope not . . .'

Guilt churns inside me. As far as animal cruelty goes, this dog says it all – she's thin, scared, trembling, yet her tail still wags, hopeful, trusting. I can't believe we left her behind a fortnight ago; there is no way I can ignore her now.

'We're taking her,' I whisper. 'We have to, Lawrie!'

He looks at me in the moonlight, his blue eyes unreadable. Two weeks ago he would have curled his lip, said something harsh and cutting about sticking to the plan, but we've both changed a lot in that time. We have rescued two ponies and helped to bring a third into the world, and this morning I woke in front of a long-dead fire with Lawrie's hand in mine. My cheeks burn at the memory.

Lawrie nods calmly and drops to his knees to untie the rope, whispering softly to the dog as he struggles with the knot.

❀❀❀❀❀❀❀❀❀❀❀❀❀❀❀❀❀❀❀❀❀❀❀❀

I am watching from the shadows when suddenly a flashlight flares and a shot rings out, splitting the night in two.

'I'm OK,' Lawrie whispers. 'Are you? Get back, quick, so he can't see you!'

My heart thumps so hard it feels like it might burst right out of me, and I can barely breathe. I edge back into the darkness, leading the ponies out of sight, round the corner, behind an outbuilding.

A tall figure is raking the flashlight across the stable yard, and I make out James Seddon, shotgun in hand, his face a tight, cold mask of fury.

'What the hell are you doing, Lawrie?' he roars. 'Leave the dog be and get in the house! I thought you were one of those blasted burglars!'

Lawrie's eyes flicker to me once more, and I creep another step backwards, my heart pounding. The ponies clatter back with me, snuffling, shaking their heads, their breath hanging in the night air like smoke.

I don't understand what's going on, how Seddon knows Lawrie's name, why he's ordering him to get in the house; my head is too scrambled to even try to make sense of

246

✿✿✿✿✿✿✿✿✿✿✿✿✿✿✿✿✿✿✿✿✿✿✿✿✿

it. All I know is that James Seddon is striding towards us in the darkness, his shotgun swinging. I have never been so terrified in my life.

I watch Lawrie's fingers fumble as the dog whimpers and cowers.

'What's going on?' Seddon growls. 'I've told you before to leave that dog alone! She's not a pet, she's a guard dog, and not even a very good one – useless mutt didn't raise the alarm when those thugs took my ponies . . .'

Lawrie abandons the rope and tugs at the dog's collar. It unbuckles suddenly and the skinny mongrel lurches away from Seddon's grip, yelping with fear, running past me in the darkness. Startled, the ponies snort and huff and sidestep, clattering away from the outbuilding, and abruptly Seddon's flashlight swoops over us all, trapping us in the dazzling light.

He laughs, and the sick, harsh sound of it turns my bones to water.

'What's this?' he enquires. 'Don't tell me, a little rescue party! It's starting to make sense now. You took the others too, didn't you? To spite me . . .'

'She wasn't involved,' Lawrie mutters, nodding at me.

❀❀❀❀❀❀❀❀❀❀❀❀❀❀❀❀❀❀❀❀❀❀❀

'Not the first time. And this was my idea too, so just let her go . . .'

'Don't worry, I know very well whose idea this was,' Seddon growls. 'You're a useless, pathetic excuse for a boy. I've tried to teach you how to have a backbone, how to be a man, but I can see that mere discipline won't do it. You need to be broken, just like the horses – you come from bad stock, you see. You're a loser, a waster, just like your dad.'

Lawrie tries to run but Seddon grabs him, hauling him back, throwing him roughly on to the ground. I think I am going to be sick; nausea seeps through me in waves, making me dizzy.

'Shhh, shhh,' I croon to the ponies, trying to calm their panic. 'Steady, now . . .'

A light goes on up at the house and a woman and child appear in the courtyard. The woman is pretty, with expensive clothes and carefully styled hair; the child is in pyjamas, sleepy and rumpled, but I recognize her instantly as the frightened girl I saw a fortnight ago.

'James?' the woman falters, pulling a mobile from her pocket. 'What's going on? Who is that? Shall I call the police?'

248

'It's Lawrie!' the child shrieks.

Lawrie pulls free, struggling to his feet, but Seddon is too fast for him; furious, he throws Lawrie against the outbuilding wall and he slumps down, gasping, clutching his arm.

'Leave him *alone!*' the woman yells, running across the yard, the child at her heels.

Seddon turns, shouting that the three of them are worthless, ungrateful trash, and before I can understand what's happening he lashes out, slapping the woman so hard that a river of blood slides down from her pink-glossed lips.

Fury floods my body and logic deserts me. I run forward with the horses, yelling. Terrified, they drag free of my grip, bucking and rearing. The skinny dog appears from the shadows, barking madly, baring her teeth at Seddon, and in the chaos the chestnut pony rears again, catching Seddon on the temple so that he reels back awkwardly, falling to the ground.

We are running then, the child's small, cold hand in mine, the woman holding Lawrie as he clutches his damaged arm. 'The car,' she gasps. 'Head for the car – I have the keys!'

❀ ❀

We race across the stable yard towards the looming shape of a four-wheel drive parked on the driveway leading down to the road. The doors flash red in the darkness, unlocking, and we bundle inside, the skinny dog too.

'Quick, Mum, he's coming!' Lawrie says, and the engine roars and there's a screech of gravel and we're driving into the darkness, away from there.

27

'Is . . . is everyone OK?' Lawrie's mum asks, her voice shaking.

Somehow, everybody is. Lawrie's mum drives slowly through the darkened lanes. I can tell it's an effort for her to keep the car steady.

'We're going the wrong way,' Lawrie says after a minute. 'We have to go to Minehead, Mum, to the police . . . we have no choice this time!'

'I can't,' she whispers, and I can hear the fear in her voice. 'We can't . . .'

My head is starting to unscramble the jigsaw pieces; a moody, secretive boy who hates bullies, the little sister, a sense of amazement that stepdads could actually be cool. This is why Lawrie was feeding Caramel the first night

❀❀❀❀❀❀❀❀❀❀❀❀❀❀❀❀❀❀❀❀❀❀❀❀❀

I went to Blue Downs House, how he knew about Spirit – and why he hates Seddon so much.

He lives with him.

'Drive to my place,' I say, taking charge. 'You're heading that way, and it's not far. You'll be safe there, I promise.'

Eventually the car limps to a halt on the gravel at Tanglewood, and I jump out and lean on the doorbell long enough to make lights spring on all over the house. By the time I have settled Lawrie, his mum and his sister in the warm kitchen and coaxed the frightened mongrel inside too, Mum and Paddy appear in the doorway in PJs and dressing gowns. My sisters crowd behind them on the staircase, wide-eyed.

'What on earth . . . Coco?' Paddy demands, but Mum just surveys the scene and puts the kettle on, fetching warm water and a clean flannel to bathe the woman's face.

'I'm Charlotte, and this is Paddy,' Mum says, matter-of-factly. 'Your name is . . . ?'

'Sandra Marshall,' the woman says, wincing as the warm water touches her broken skin. 'Sandy. These are my children, Lawrie and Jasmine . . .'

'Lawrie's my friend from school,' I add. 'We were trying to rescue some ponies and it all got out of hand . . .'

'Way to go, little sis,' Honey says. 'Stepping into my shoes as the rebel-rouser already? I haven't even gone yet!'

'Honey, shhh, this is serious,' Mum says. 'What exactly happened here?'

'I don't know,' I tell her. 'But I think Lawrie's arm might be broken and the horses have gone and –'

'He hit my mum,' Jasmine says in a tiny voice. 'And he shot his gun!'

'Who did?' Mum echoes. 'Sandy, who did this to you?'

The whole story comes out then, the bits I know already and the bits I could only guess at; about the shotgun, the slap, the stolen horses, about a whole year of intimidation and bullying for Lawrie and his family.

They came to Somerset a year ago when Sandy found work with James Seddon's holiday-let business. Soon Seddon was dating her and moved the whole family in with him. He made them feel special with gifts and days out and endless promises . . . but before long he began to control everything they did. When Seddon

253

❀❀❀❀❀❀❀❀❀❀❀❀❀❀❀❀❀❀❀❀❀❀❀

began to show a darker side, a cruel, bullying streak, Lawrie had to stand by and watch as fear pulled his family apart.

'Where do the ponies come into all this?' Mum asks. 'This rescue you mentioned, Coco?'

'Seddon was the one who bought Caramel,' I explain. 'I went to see if she was all right and she really, really wasn't. Seddon drove her to exhaustion, made Jasmine watch until she fell down in the mud, crying. So I took Caramel away . . . me and Lawrie. We had to. There was another pony too, a mare in foal. We hid them on the moors, and when Lawrie told me Seddon had bought more ponies we tried to take them too, but the dog barked and Seddon came after us with a shotgun and it all went wrong . . .'

My sisters have moved into the kitchen, perched on the countertops or leaning against the Aga. Paddy has slipped out of the room. Jasmine has fallen asleep in Sandy's arms, Lawrie is curled up with the skinny mongrel.

Mum touches Sandy's hand. 'You have to call the police,' she says gently. 'You know that, don't you?'

'I can't,' she whispers. 'I really can't . . .'

'You don't have to,' Paddy says, as he comes through the kitchen door. 'They're already on their way.'

The night goes crazy. Paramedics arrive and decide that Lawrie's arm isn't broken, that Sandy's cuts will heal and hopefully not scar; the police take a statement from Lawrie's mum, ask if she wishes to press charges, and dispatch officers to bring Seddon down to the station. It's daybreak by the time all that is done. My sisters have gone back to bed, and Lawrie and Jasmine are asleep in one of the guest rooms.

'You and I need a little talk,' Mum says, catching my arm as I try to slope upstairs. 'I'm glad you brought Lawrie and Sandy and Jasmine here, but . . . what on earth have you been thinking, Coco? Stealing ponies, wandering around on the moors in the dark? That was dangerous . . . I mean, really dangerous!'

Her eyes fill with tears and instantly I am flooded with guilt. Mum is right, of course – I may have acted with the best intentions, but still, I have broken the law and lied and taken so many risks that it has become second nature. Suddenly, it doesn't look daring or brave so much as downright foolhardy.

'Sorry, Mum,' I whisper. 'I just . . . didn't know what else to do!'

Mum wipes her eyes. 'You could have talked to me,' she says. 'I'd have listened, Coco, you know that, don't you? Together, we could have worked something out. But I really don't think I could bear to have another daughter in trouble. The family seems to be unravelling before my very eyes . . .'

'No, Mum!' I protest. 'That's not true! We're the best family in the world! We may not be perfect, but we're still pretty amazing, and that's thanks to you and Paddy. I'm fine, I promise, really I am! I'm so, so sorry!'

But Mum is crying again, and all I can do is put my arms round her and hold her close and promise I will talk to her if there's anything, anything at all, I am worried about in future. And I mean it. Forget boys and make-up and cramps and mood swings, this is what growing up is all about – learning from your mistakes, daring to admit that you don't know everything, and that sometimes, just maybe, you get things wrong.

It's hard. There's an ache inside my chest and I want to cry and argue and yell, but I won't, I can't. I am going

❀ ❀

to learn, listen, change. I am going to make Mum proud. I hold her tight and promise that everything will be OK.

In the end, Lawrie and his family stay with us for two weeks. Sandy helps out in the chocolate workshop, and it turns out she is a whizz at organizing and getting things to run smoothly. Pretty soon, the order is back on track.

As well as the police, the RSPCA are investigating Seddon, and the *Exmoor Gazette* runs a story on it all. Seddon has been shamed into handing the two newest ponies back to their original owner, while Jean and Roy at the stables take on Spirit and Star. Sheba the dog has gained weight and her fur looks glossy and healthy. She curls up in Fred's basket at night and runs rings round the garden with him during the day.

Lawrie and I are Year Eight heroes for all of five minutes, then targets for endless teasing about whether we are/aren't an item. For the record, we are not, but Lawrie has chilled out now his mum is away from Seddon; the moody, chippy veneer has dropped away to reveal a quiet, gentle boy who opens up a little more each day.

He surprises me sometimes. When I show Jasmine how

❀❀❀❀❀❀❀❀❀❀❀❀❀❀❀❀❀❀❀❀❀❀❀❀

to make my secret Coco Caramel cupcakes he joins in, whizzing up flour and eggs and butter and sugar; he sits beside me in the old oak tree, listening to my violin practice, looking at the stars, talking about the past, the future, a hundred different versions of each.

Eventually, of course, the future becomes the present.

The chocolate order is finished, the last consignment driven away. Sandy makes plans to go back to Kendal, staying with her parents until she can find a job and a flat. Jasmine and Lawrie will go back to their old schools, putting the past behind them.

I am pleased for the Marshalls, really I am, but the news leaves me feeling strangely deflated. On the day they leave, I sit in the old oak, legs swinging, gloomy. I have baked panda-face cupcakes for Jasmine, packed a bag with dog chews for Sheba, painted a good-luck card for all of them. Still, it feels like I am crying inside.

Lawrie comes out of the house and down through the garden, hauling himself up into the branches beside me.

'I don't want you to go,' I confess. 'I will miss you, Lawrie Marshall.'

'I'll miss you,' he counters. 'It's for the best, though.

The further Mum is from Seddon the better. Maybe things will be OK for your family too, now?'

'Sure they will. Your mum had the chocolate workshop running like clockwork. I can't believe we made that deadline after all!'

'With time to spare,' he tells me. 'Mum loved it. It's been like watching her wake up, start to believe in herself again – thanks to Charlotte and Paddy. And you, obviously.'

'What did I do?'

He shrugs. 'Without you, I'd never have dared stand up to Seddon. He'd knocked the fight out of us – all I could do was look out for Mum and Jas, make sure the animals were fed. Then you turned up with your mad plans and suddenly everything was different, we were in the middle of this big adventure. You gave me hope. OK, at first I thought you were a little bit crazy . . .'

'I am a little bit crazy,' I agree.

He grins. 'I know. I got to like it, after a while. It's been so long since I had a proper friend, and I think . . . I know . . . well, you're probably my best friend. Maybe more than a friend . . .'

❀❀❀❀❀❀❀❀❀❀❀❀❀❀❀❀❀❀❀❀❀❀❀❀❀

I don't see it coming.

I have noticed the way he looks at me sometimes, his blue eyes sad and searching, noticed a crackle of energy between us sometimes when we touch by accident. I've laughed off my friends' suggestions that he fancies me, but I'd be lying if I said I hadn't wondered if he did. I'd be lying too, if I said I hadn't thought about Lawrie a little bit, dreamed even.

Still, I panic when he leans towards me, his fingers stroking my cheek, his lips brushing mine. I almost jump out of my skin, and that is not a good plan when you are six feet above the ground, sitting in an old oak tree.

I am pretty sure it's not the reaction Lawrie was hoping for.

I put my hand out, touch his cheek, his lips. His skin is cold beneath my fingers, but his lips are soft and warm.

'Hey,' I whisper. 'Lawrie, you're my best friend too, but . . . well, I don't think I'm ready for anything more right now. Is that OK?'

'I guess,' he says. 'I'll wait. I'll come back one day, I promise, and we'll both be older then and things will be different. Yeah?'

❀❀❀❀❀❀❀❀❀❀❀❀❀❀❀❀❀❀❀❀❀❀

'I hope so,' I tell him. 'We can write, can't we? And email, maybe.'

'Definitely. Listen, Coco, I hate goodbyes,' he says. 'Besides, I know we'll meet again. But if we don't, for whatever reason, there's one thing you have to know. I will never forget you, Coco Tanberry. Never.'

He slides down from the oak tree and walks away, and by the time the taxi arrives to take them to the station I am playing the violin, thinking of a boy with sad eyes, warm lips, unruly hair that falls across his face.

I guess I hate goodbyes as well.

A week ago we took Honey to Heathrow to catch her flight to Sydney. Honey looked small, lost, alone as she walked out through the security gates, and I panicked suddenly that we might lose her forever. Living with a stormcloud like Honey has never been easy, but I don't think I will ever get used to her not being around. In some ways, this has been the worst week of my life.

In other ways, it has been the best.

As I play, a pony comes towards me through the long grass, a rough-coated bay with a wild, dark mane and tail, her eyes soft and shining. Caramel watches me solemnly

❀❀❀❀❀❀❀❀❀❀❀❀❀❀❀❀❀❀❀❀❀❀❀❀❀

for a while, ears pricked as I play. It turns out that she really was Jasmine's birthday pony, but of course there will be no room for her at Jas and Lawrie's gran's house. Fitting three people and a skinny mongrel in is one thing; finding space for an Exmoor pony is something else entirely.

'You sent me cupcakes and jasmine flowers,' the little girl explained to me last week. 'Before you even met me. That was kind. And you saved Caramel and kept her safe, so . . . will you look after her for me now? Please?'

I promised that I would.

Just a few weeks ago I thought that if I had Caramel, all my troubles would be over; she's mine now, pretty much, but I have a feeling my troubles are just beginning. I said this to Honey at the airport last week, and she laughed and told me that I'd be fine, that I was just growing up. Well, maybe.

I slide down to the ground, put my violin away and take Caramel's halter, leading her up to the stable she shares with Humbug the sheep. I saddle her carefully, adjust her reins and swing up on to her back, and together we walk out through the field gate heading down, slowly, towards the beach.

✿✿✿✿✿✿✿✿✿✿✿✿✿✿✿✿✿✿✿✿✿✿✿✿

Caramel tosses her head in the wind and skitters a little as her hooves sink into the sand. We turn to face the vast shimmering expanse of ocean, now streaked with red and gold as the sun drops steadily lower in the sky, and I think of another afternoon, riding Caramel across the moors with Lawrie's arms round me. Then I shake the memory free and press my heels in gently and we bound forward into a canter, out along the beach, heads down, happy, glad to be alive.

Dear Honey,

If you're reading this note you are probably at the departure gate or maybe actually up in the clouds already, on the way to Australia. It's just to say some of the things I couldn't say out loud. I didn't want to cry, and I didn't want us to argue. So here goes.

a) *You may be the most annoying big sister in the world, but I am going to miss you.*

b) *I know it's not forever but I think you are making a BIG mistake. It is bad enough having a dad on the other side of the planet without losing your sister too.*

c) *Things won't be the same without you. (They will probably be a lot quieter, but I don't care. I still wish you weren't going.)*

Your favourite sister,
Coco xxx

1

I smile and fold the note neatly, putting it back into the pocket of my shoulder bag. My little sister is crazy, and I will miss her too, but she knows as well as I do that my days at Tanglewood are over. I've messed up one time too many. What can I say? Getting a friend to hack into the school computer system to fake my grades and school reports was not my best move, and getting caught and expelled kind of sealed the deal.

I needed a one-way ticket out of there, and Dad stepped up to the mark and provided me with one. A ticket to Australia, a new start, a way out of the mess my life has been lately. Who wouldn't have said yes?

It takes twenty-three hours to fly from London Heathrow to Sydney, and that is a very long time to be stuck in cattle-class on a plane. I eat the weird, pre-packed dinner-on-a-tray and ask for a glass of wine to go with it, but the stewardess just rolls her eyes and hands me an orange juice. Everything tastes of sawdust anyway, so I don't much care. We stop off in Singapore for the plane to refuel, but apart from a brief walk around the airport I don't get to actually see anything of the place. And then we're back on the plane and the other passengers yawn and tip their seats back and huddle down under thin fleece blankets with funny little eye-masks on, and the lights go down on life as I know it.

I am too excited to sleep. Australia – land of sunshine, surf, opportunities! I take out a pocket sketchbook and doodle pictures of myself flying through the stars, wearing a sundress and feathered wings and my vintage high-heeled boots.

I put on my headphones and watch two movies in a row, then I flick on my overhead light and read two magazines. Like I said, it's a long flight. I go to the bathroom and walk up and down the aisle for exercise a few times like it tells you to do on long-haul flights, but the eye-rolly stewardess gives me a very sour look, so I sit down again and try to be patient.

Maybe I actually do fall asleep, for a minute or two at least, because, the next thing I know, the lights snap on again and the sky outside is pink with the promise of dawn. It's almost morning, Sydney time. The stewardess hands me a sawdust-flavoured shrink-wrapped breakfast, but I am so excited I can't eat a thing, and then we are buckling up the seatbelts ready for landing. Finally.

When I step out on to those aeroplane steps and take my first ever look at a Sydney daybreak, I am so brimful of happiness I think I might burst.

Dad is waiting for me at Arrivals, tanned and smiling, effortlessly cool in a grey linen suit. He has to be forty, easy, but he doesn't look it. As always, he draws a few admiring glances from women of a certain age, but Dad's grin is all for me. I run towards him, pulling my wheely suitcase behind me, and he scoops me up in a big bear hug, laughing.

'How's my best girl?' he asks, and I am so happy I could burst. I've waited a very long time to hear those words.

'Breakfast?' he suggests, swinging up my heavy suitcase as if it weighs nothing. 'Those flights are a killer, and plane food is the pits. Let's get you something decent!'

I am not especially hungry, but I would follow my dad just about anywhere right now, so I trail after him into the leafy enclosure of an upmarket airport restaurant. He orders for both of us, something fancy with poached eggs and hollandaise sauce, freshly squeezed orange juice, croissants, jam.

'So,' he says, leaning back as the waitress hurries off with our order. 'Here we go. A new start in Australia! What's going on, Honey Tanberry?'

I raise my chin. I have messed up; I know it. I have made so many mistakes it's hard to know where to begin. It started with me skipping school, telling lies, staying out all night with a fairground boy called Kes and his unsuitable friends. Mum was majorly upset about that, and I was glad. Yes, Kes was older than me; yes, he was kind of rough round the edges; yes, he was trouble. So what? I happen to like trouble.

I am good at it too. You could say I have trouble down to a fine art. I lied, I cheated, I stopped studying. Then came the bit I mentioned, about persuading a friend to hack the school computer system and 'adjust' my grades. We got found out. I ended up with Social Services on my case, with Mum crying and my sisters yelling and my stupid stepdad Paddy raking a hand through his hair and looking at me sadly as if I was the one who pulled our happy family to bits, and not him.

Yeah, well, we all know that isn't how it happened.

It doesn't matter, because in the end I've got what I wanted – the fresh start to beat them all. A new life, with Dad, in Australia.

I have done my research. I know that Australia is beautiful, sunshiney, unspoilt. It's the perfect place for new beginnings. It's also the place where Britain once shipped its convicts, long ago.

I reckon I will fit right in.

'I take it you were struggling, living with your mum?' Dad says, sipping a latte. 'Not all happy families, huh?'

'We haven't been a family for ages,' I tell him flatly. 'Not since you left.'

Dad just laughs, but it's true. He knows I don't blame him – it's what happened afterwards that did the damage.

When Dad left, that whole family thing slipped through our fingers and shattered like glass. We tried to pick up the pieces, put them together again, but we just couldn't. The only one who could have done it was Dad, and before he got the chance Paddy pitched up with his hateful, boyfriend-stealing daughter, Cherry, and that was that. Dad took a transfer out to Australia and my dream that he'd come back to us some day bit the dust big style. One broken family, no longer any hope for repairs.

'Life moves on,' Dad says lightly. 'I know I haven't always been able to be there for you. I can see you've found it tough, these last few years.'

'Just a bit.'

It's not like I didn't try my best – I threw confetti at the wedding, smiled at Paddy across the breakfast table, resisted the urge to slap Cherry's lying, cheating face. I pretended it was all OK, but it wasn't, and sooner or later I knew the game of Let's Pretend would fall apart.

It all blew up, and things were looking pretty bad – then Dad chucked me a lifeline and now here I am, shipped out to Australia, a modern-day convict girl. I will be attending a private school that sounds like a cross between bad-girl boot camp and hippy-dippy wholemeal heaven with counselling and one-to-one support to help me get a handful of exams after all.

'Things will be better here,' Dad says. 'A fresh start. You're my girl, Honey – I know you can make a go of it, turn things around. Right?'

'Right!' I agree.

Well, maybe.

I am just happy to be here, with a clean slate and a last, last chance to get my life on track. I am determined to make it work. Call me cynical, but sometimes it is easier to walk away from a messed-up life than to stick around and patch things up. It doesn't mean I don't love my mum and sisters – I do. I just can't be a part of the new-look family they've put together.

Fresh starts . . . Dad has always been good at those, and I plan to be too.

'You're a lot like me, you know, Honey,' Dad tells me between mouthfuls of breakfast. 'I was a bit of a rebel in my time. I had a few ups and downs, a few changes of school before I settled down. We're alike, you and I.'

I smile. I want to be like Dad – who wouldn't? He is dramatic, confident, charismatic. He has this magic about him – when he looks at you, you feel like you're the only person in the whole wide world. You feel special, chosen, golden.

I felt this way all the time when I was a kid – I was Dad's favourite. Then he left, and everything turned to dust. Without Dad, everything at Tanglewood was cold and empty and hollow.

It will be different here.

Dad is telling me about the house, the pool, the nearby beach. He is explaining how Sydney is the most beautiful city he knows, how he will help me explore it, how I will learn to love it too.

I almost miss it when Dad mentions, ever so casually, that it won't be just me and him in the fancy beachside bungalow with the outdoor pool. It will be me, him and his girlfriend, Emma. My ears buzz and for a moment everything seems foggy, cold. It could be jet lag, but I don't think so. Through the fog, Dad's words worm themselves into my brain.

'Emma's lovely,' he says carelessly. 'You'll get along great!'

Emma. The name rings a bell, but I think it's just the situation that's familiar. Disappointment curdles in my belly, sharp and sour. I have spent years without my dad, and I really, really don't want to have to share him now.

It looks like I have flown halfway around the world to escape an annoying stepdad, only to have acquired some kind of stepmum.

That was never part of the plan.

A gorgeous new series by

Cathy Cassidy

The Chocolate Box GIRLS

Cherry:
Dark almond eyes, skin the colour of milky coffee, wild imagination, feisty, fun . . .

Skye:
Wavy blonde hair, blue eyes, smiley, individual, kind . . .

Summer:
Slim, graceful, pretty, loves to dance, determined, a girl with big dreams . . .

Coco:
Blue eyes, fair hair, freckles, a tomboy who loves animals and wants to change the world . . .

Honey:
Willowy, blonde, beautiful, arty and out of control, a rebel . . .

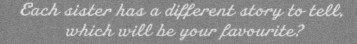

Each sister has a different story to tell, which will be your favourite?

Cherry Costello is...

shy, quiet, always on the outside . . .
sometimes finds it hard to separate
truth from fiction

14 years old

Born: Glasgow

Mum: Kiko

Dad: Paddy

Looks: small; slim; coffee-coloured skin;
straight, dark hair with a fringe, often
worn in little bunches

Style: bright skinny jeans, T-shirts,
anything with a Japanese theme

Loves: dreaming, stories, cherry blossom,
Irn-Bru, gypsy caravans

Prize possessions: kimono, parasol,
Japanese fan, photo of her mum
from long ago

Dreams: of being part of a family

Skye Tanberry is ...

friendly, eccentric, individual, imaginative

13 years old - Summer's identical twin

Born: Kitnor

Mum: Charlotte

Dad: Greg

Looks: shoulder-length blonde hair,
blue eyes, big grin

Style: floppy hats and vintage dresses,
scarves and shoes

Loves: history, horoscopes,
dreaming, drawing

Prize possessions: her collection
of vintage dresses and the fossil
she once found on the beach

Dreams: of travelling back in
time to see what the past
was really like . . .

     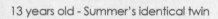 

www.cathycassidy.com

Summer Tanberry is ...

quiet, confident, pretty, popular, and very serious about dance

13 years old - Skye's identical twin

Born: Kitnor

Mum: Charlotte

Dad: Greg

Looks: long blonde hair, always tied back in braids or a neat ballerina bun; blue eyes; moves gracefully

Style: anything pink . . . neat, pretty, fashionable clothes and dance-wear

Loves: dancing, especially ballet

Prize possessions: pointe shoes and tutu

Dreams: of going to the Royal Ballet School, becoming a professional dancer and one day running her own ballet school

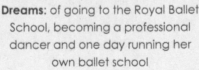

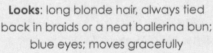

Coco Tanberry is ...

cheeky, energetic, friendly,
adventurous, crazy about animals

12 years old

Born: Kilnor

Mum: Charlotte

Dad: Greg

Looks: chin-length wavy blonde hair,
always tangled; blue eyes; freckles;
big grin

Style: tomboy: jeans, T-shirt, always
messy and dishevelled

Loves: animals, climbing trees,
swimming in the sea

Prize possessions: Fred the dog
and the ducks

Dreams: of having a llama,
a donkey and a parrot

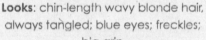

Honey Tanberry is ...

a drama queen: moody, selfish, often sad . . . but also bright, charming, organized and sweet .

15 years old

Born: London

Mum: Charlotte

Dad: Greg

Looks: long, ringletty blonde hair that reaches to her waist; blue eyes; creamy skin; tall; slim

Style: cool: little print dresses, strappy sandals, shades, shorts and T-shirts

Loves: drawing, painting, fashion, music . . . and Shay Fletcher

Prize possessions: hair, diary, sketchbook, turret bedroom

Dreams: of being a model, actress or fashion designer

www.cathycassidy.com